PRAISE FOR A'NDREA J. WILSON'S

Wife 101

"This is one of the best books I've read this year. I found myself laughing and shaking my head all the way through it! I can't wait to read the follow up, Husband 101, which will focus on a man's point of view. Great job, A'ndrea!"
  - *New York Times® Bestselling Author Mary Monroe*

"More than anything, I appreciated the actual class lessons included in the book. I found myself stopping and doing the lessons right along with the main character and re-evaluating my role as a wife and homemaker - my first ministry. As a result of reading this book, some concrete changes have been made in my life and in my household."
  – *Essence® Bestselling Author Michelle Stimpson*

"Wilson has written a story that transcends all boundaries. Wife 101 is a teaching and learning tool for anyone wanting to improve on their relationships. The character development is steady and believable while the storyline intriguing...This book is clearly winner that I will be purchasing as gifts for friends that cross my path. Definitely a top 5 read for 2012."

  - *M. Bruner (DeltaReviewer)*

"Best-Seller in the making! One of the best fiction reads I've come across lately! I love the fact that this book now has a workbook component to be used as a discussion tool and I can't wait to see/hear the feedback from others who have read Wife 101!"

– Joy Turner, Author of Content Where I am

"A'ndrea Wilson has accomplished what many Christian authors fail at - she writes a Christian fiction story which is completely realistic and relatable. Wilson keeps an equal mix of fiction and Biblical references without one overshadowing the other."

– Tiffany Craig (Read It All Reviews)

"Wilson offers a good balance of information and entertainment. While the main character Amber was highly successful, she was down to earth and relatable, dealing with struggles common to women. With a relatable, likable character, it's easy for readers to have a vested interest in the story and Amber's plight."

– Ms. Toni (OOSA Online Book Club)

Husband 101

Books by A'ndrea J. Wilson

Wife 101

The Wife 101 Workbook

The Husband 101 Workbook

Ready & ABLE Teens: Ebony's Bad Habit

Ready & ABLE Teens: Desiree Dishes the Dirt

Kiss & Tell: Releasing Expectations

The Things We Said We Would Never Do

My Business His Way: Wisdom & Inspiration for Entrepreneurs

Collaborations

Love Said Not So (Anthology)

He Loves Me, He Loves Me Not (with Twilla Robinson-Booker)

Writing as Janell

Spell

Grave

Vanity

Husband 101

A'NDREA J. WILSON

WWW.DIVINEGARDENPRESS.COM

Published by Divine Garden Press
P.O. Box 371
Soperton, GA 30457
www.divinegardenpress.com

ISBN-13: 978-0615695082
ISBN-10: 0615695086
Library of Congress Control Number: 2012949051
Cover Photography: The Snappy Diva|www.thesnappydiva.com
Cover Design: A'ndrea J. Wilson
Interior Design: A'ndrea J. Wilson
Author Photo: Antonio Cleveland

to mom & dad
who showed me that marriage is <u>still</u> a lifetime commitment

Acknowledgements

It takes a village to write a good book. I am forever grateful to my village, the people who have positively influenced both the writing of Husband 101 and my career as an author.

God: I am still trying to figure this thing out; how to worship You with my life. Thank You for choosing me again, and using me to touch lives through the words I write and say. This is Your book, I am just the vessel.

Pastor Kathleen Wilson (Mom): I can never thank you enough for a lifetime of love and support. You are always close to my heart and in my thoughts!

Adele Brinkley (Editor): I value your wisdom and insight. I always feel a zillion times better about my work once it comes back from spending time with you. A thousand thanks.

Norlita Brown, Lynn Pinder, & Vanessa Davis (Proofreaders): You ladies stepped up to the plate and did me the honor of blessing my manuscript with your critical eyes and minds. Thank you all for supporting me, for your honesty, and for your time.

Family & Friends: There is no way I could even begin to list all of the friends and family who have been there for me in some shape or form throughout the years so I will just say a BIG thank you to all of you, you know who you are. A special thanks to Darius Harmon, Kesha Lee Wilson, Tanisha Smith, Amelia Speaks, and Sharon Bruner. Thank you to the finer women of Zeta Phi Beta Sorority, Inc. and Chi Pi Zeta Chapter (Hinesville, GA).

Authors: Thanks to every author who I have connected with that has encouraged me to stay focused and keep writing. Mary Monroe, you are such a sweetheart and I thank you for taking the time to look out for me. I value your friendship and hearty appetite. TaNisha Webb, who would have thought a one year wait on a Christmas CD would have turned into such a treasured friendship? Thanks for your honesty and knowledge. You always push me to be better. Laura Parker Castoro, you have been a wonderful mentor and a pleasure to learn from. Thanks for hanging out with me. Michelle Stimpson, such a kindred spirit. Thanks for traveling this road of marital redemption. It can get lonely along the way and it's so nice to walk with a friend. Carmen Calhoun, our day is soon. Daddy is about to do the much, much more. Hold on! Joy Turner, just keep laughing and let me be me. Thanks for the love! Thanks to M-PACT Writers and Christian Authors on Tour for the support and collaboration.

Book Clubs: A HUGE thanks to all of the book clubs that have read Wife 101 and hopefully will read Husband 101. Off the top of my head, thanks to OOSA Online Book Club, Exquisite Ladies Book Club, Reader's Block Book Club, WOS, Reading with a Purpose, Candler County Book Club, Treutlen County Library Book Club, Pages of Grace, African American Women of Destiny, and KC Girlfriends Book Club. Book Clubs: please let me know if you are reading any of my books. I would love to hear from you!

Book Reviewers: Thanks to literary industry book reviewers who have taken the time to read a book in the Wife 101 series, J. L. Whitehead, Monique Bruner, Mz Tiffany Divine, Urban Reviews, Tiffany Craig, ARC, and OOSA. Thanks to all of the readers who have also taken the time to review my books on Amazon, Goodreads, or any other review site.

Readers: I write for God, and I write for you. Thank you for purchasing my books and supporting my dreams. You have encouraged me through your emails, Facebook messages, Tweets, and purchases. A book is nothing without readers, so from the bottom of my heart, thank you and happy reading!

A'ndrea

Lesson 1: Temptation Is Everywhere

Be well balanced (temperate, sober of mind), be vigilant and cautious at all times; for that enemy of yours, the devil, roams around like a lion roaring [in fierce hunger], seeking someone to seize upon and devour. (I Peter 5:8)

What most women don't seem to understand about men is that society is set up for us to fail at relationships. Many of us want to be good husbands, boyfriends, and fathers, but from the moment we wake up in the morning to the minute we lie down at night, something in this world pushes us to take an alternative path from the one our hearts know we should be on. These days, I couldn't turn on the television, listen to the radio, or even go to work without some form of temptation whispering sweet nothings into the openings of the vulnerable parts of my mind.

The woman who sat across from me in my office was a perfect example of temptation in high heels. Merely one hour after I kissed my still newlywed wife goodbye and left our cozy Atlanta home to come to the realty company that we owned, another woman who considered herself a client of that same realty was openly flirting with me. It was apparent to me that the woman was attracted to me, but for the sake of business *and my marriage*, I brushed off her flattery and maintained my focus.

"Mr. Hayes," she said while crossing her right leg over her left, allowing my eyes access to the parts of her thighs that weren't covered by her miniskirt or knee-high boots.

"Please call me Eric," I said quickly, making sure I kept my eyes looking directly into hers and not allowing them to roam as another man would.

She smiled charmingly. "Well then, Eric, I've heard a lot of great things about Hayes & Ross Realty, especially as it relates to commercial properties. As you know, my fitness centers are in most of the major US cities: New York, L.A., Miami, Chicago, and D.C. We even have a location in Japan. I know it's time to bring Flawless Fitness to 'Hotlanta.' I put the word out a couple of months ago, and people are already breaking their necks to get memberships. I just need a prime location, preferably something in Midtown. If we can escrow by the end of the year, I can do presales on gym memberships in January when everyone is making their New Year's weight loss resolutions."

Jacqueline Johnson's eyes lit up as she continued to ruminate about her business plans. She reminded me a lot of my wife, Amber Ross-Hayes, ambitious with a capital A.

"Ms. Johnson, I–"

She interrupted. "Call me Jay."

I chuckled and nodded. "Jay, I am positive that we will be able to help you find a home in Atlanta for your business."

"Wonderful!" She stood up, her Angola sweater stopped mid-drift exposing her sculpted six-pack abdominals and a jeweled belly ring. She slid her leather jacket on and took a few steps closer to my desk.

Peering down at me with a sly expression, she said, "I have no doubts that *you're* the right man for the job."

I gave her a nervous grin. "Thank you for your vote of confidence. I will be in touch soon."

She winked at me and sashayed out of my office and down the hall, her waist-length, jet black braids swishing from side to side as she walked.

I sat back in my chair and let out a deep sigh. The woman was trouble, but I needed her business. The realty had been given to me by my wife as a wedding gift seven months ago. Before that, I had worked for the company as an office manager. Now that I was running the company, I wanted to show Amber that I could handle being the new CEO and could take what she started and make something even bigger out of it. When Amber was in charge, the realty dealt primarily with residential properties, but I was interested in becoming more involved in the commercial sector. We had sold several smaller commercial properties over the last few months, but landing Flawless Fitness as a client was huge. If I could close this deal, other international companies would surely take notice.

"There is a God!" A masculine voice permeated through my thoughts. I looked at the entrance to my office and saw Carl, one of the real estate agents, standing there ogling Jacqueline as she exited the building. "Too bad you're married, E. I can handle that for you if you need me to."

I shook my head. "Carl, you know you're married too, right?"

"Yeah, but I've been married over ten years. I can be around a woman like that and look but not touch. You, on the other hand, are new to the game. That woman right there is what you call a home wrecker, a *miss-stress*! Mm hmm! I can tell that she has broken up a few marriages. Yep! She ain't doing all that twisting for nothing. She has targeted you as her next victim. Next!" he yelled and then broke into laughter.

I waved him away. "Whatever, man. Aren't you supposed to be showing someone a house or doing something productive rather than bothering me?"

"Nope. I got a walk-through at noon, but until then, I'm here with you. And don't try to change the subject. All I'm saying is that you might need to have her work with another agent. I'm willing to help because I've seen Amber angry, and it's *not* a pretty sight."

"Why would Amber get angry? She understands business. This is *just* business."

"Come on, E. Don't play dumb with me. If Amber ever sees Jacqueline flirting with you, business or no business, she is going to flip out. All women get crazy when it comes to other women. You've got sisters; you already know how women are!"

"Carl, thanks for the lesson on women, but seriously, I've got this. I love my wife, and I am not interested in Jacqueline or any other woman. I think I can handle this one, but if I need your help, I'll let you know."

"All right, man. I'll keep my cell phone close," Carl replied before laughing and walking away.

I didn't want to admit it, but I knew Carl was right. I had two sisters, and one of the things they had taught me was that women tend to become very insecure when other beautiful women are around. I wanted to believe that Amber was different, that her self-assurance didn't flee at the first sight of another pretty face, but I sensed that was not the case. Amber was special, but she was still a woman.

I sank deeper into my chair, unconsciously shaking my head in the process. This client was far too important for me to leave in the hands of Carl or another agent; I needed to manage her myself. At the same time, I didn't want any unnecessary or unexpected drama to affect the "good thing" I had going with Amber. I quietly prayed that I could get Jacqueline to behave herself while keeping Amber from knowing that Jacqueline, a.k.a. Jay, even existed.

I guess I asked God for a little too much.

Lesson 2: One Poor Choice Can Lead To A Lifetime Of Pain

Should your offspring be dispersed abroad as water brooks in the streets? [Confine yourself to your own wife] let your children be for you alone, and not the children of strangers with you.

(Proverbs 5:16-17)

"I am running out of patience. That chick's got one more time to come at me like that before I break her down! Now, I know I'm a Christian woman, but she's about to make me lose all of my religion," I heard my wife say as I walked into the house.

I stepped into the kitchen to find Amber leaning over the stove mixing spaghetti sauce while cradling the cordless phone between her right shoulder and ear. I figured she was on the phone with her partner in crime, her best friend Tisha. I was right. The phone's volume was loud, and I could make out Tisha's over-animated voice saying something about being willing to go to jail for assault.

Amber, noticing I had entered the room, spun around and greeted me with a smile. She pointed at the phone with the large wooden spoon that was in her hand then said to Tisha, "Um Hmm . . . Right . . . I know. But listen, Eric just walked in, so I'll call you back later." She hung up the phone and placed it on the counter before coming over to me and kissing me softly on the lips.

"So, who are you and Tisha getting ready to serve jail time over?" I joked once the kiss had ended.

She waved the spoon in my face, threateningly. "Lena! *Your* ex-girlfriend. The mother of *your* child."

Dunn-Dunn-Dunn-Dunnnnn! I could have sworn I heard the intro to Beethoven's "Fifth" being played in the background, or maybe it was just the wild beating of my heart.

"Lena? What did she do now?" I asked as if the answer actually mattered. Lena Henry was indeed my ex-girlfriend and the mother to my eleven-year-old daughter, Jonelle. Before my marriage to Amber, Lena acted as if I was the last man in the world she wanted to talk to, but since I'd said my wedding vows, Lena had become somewhat of a stalker. She called our house constantly, always claiming Jonelle wanted to speak to me or that Jonelle needed something for school. I believed that she was intentionally trying to irritate Amber, especially knowing that Amber was pregnant with our first child.

Amber walked back over to the stove and stirred the sauce again. "She called here talking to me like I'm slow. Gonna tell me that I need to write down her messages because you somehow never get them. I forgot to give you one message. One message three months ago, and she's acting like I rode on the short bus with the special education students. She doesn't know me, Eric. Like I told Tisha, if I wasn't pregnant and saved . . . !"

I walked up behind her and wrapped my arms around her waist affectionately. "But you are both pregnant and saved, so I can't have you fighting with Jonelle's mother or going to prison with Tisha."

I kissed her on the back of the neck and she let out a soft giggle. "I will deal with Lena," I said. "You just stop letting her and everything else stress you out. You know what the doctor–"

She stiffened. "I know. Please stop reminding me."

I sighed and kissed her once more on the neck, but she didn't respond this time, and I knew why. Although Amber had become pregnant only four months following our wedding, the pregnancy was risky. Her doctor was concerned about miscarriage due to Amber's high stress levels and high blood pressure. He recommended that Amber slow down her busy work schedule and avoid stressful situations. Asking Amber to avoid stress was like asking a Pentecostal or Baptist church not to pass around the collection plate; it wasn't going to happen.

"Sorry," I whispered into her ear. I felt her relax a bit underneath my embrace. I hated to badger her about her health, but Amber refused to follow the doctor's orders. I, however, was terrified that we would lose our child. If saving our unborn baby meant gently telling Amber to chill out, I would do what I had to do.

"I'll call Lena and see what she wanted," I said, changing the subject as I pulled away from Amber and headed towards the refrigerator. I opened the refrigerator door and peered inside despite the fact that I already knew what was in it. I guess it was just out of habit.

She turned to face me, picked the phone up from the countertop, and extended it to me. I closed the refrigerator door without retrieving anything from inside and reached out to take the phone from her hand.

"Are you planning to sign up for the Husband 101 class?" Amber asked when the phone was firmly in my possession.

"I don't know. I guess." I glanced up at her. I could tell by the look in her eyes that she was annoyed. She had been trying to get me to commit to taking the course for months now, and although it sounded like it would be somewhat interesting, I had so many other things on my mind that I just didn't feel it was the right time. Taking the class meant giving up my Monday nights for several weeks, and it was football season! What man in his right mind would schedule anything on a Monday in the fall? Not only that, but with my hopes of landing top notch commercial clients, I had to have a certain level of flexibility. What if a client could meet only on a Monday evening? I couldn't risk losing a moneymaking deal over this church-school stuff.

"Well, it starts on Monday so you need to hurry up and make a decision. Minister Martin is saving a spot for you, but I need to let him know by Sunday." Amber glared at me, waiting for me to respond. When I didn't, she sighed disappointedly and went back to preparing dinner. Feeling the tension, I walked out of the kitchen and into the living room. Since I was already in the doghouse, I figured it was a good time to call Lena back and get chewed out a bit more.

"What's up?" I greeted Lena as I heard her answer the phone.

"Oh, I see your *wife* finally gave you my message. It's about time."

"Whatever, Lena. She always gives me your messages. Look, I'm not in the mood to argue with you tonight, so what's up? What did you call me for?"

She paused, seemingly searching for an excuse before saying, "I called to tell you that Jonelle isn't going to be able to see you this weekend."

"What? Why not?"

"Something came up."

"Something always comes up! Lena, this is not right! You're not being fair."

She sucked her teeth. "So! Life ain't fair. You'll get over it."

"But I haven't seen her in almost a month. Please don't do this to me, Lena."

"Like I said, something came up."

"You know what? Keep it up and I will take you to court for custody."

She laughed, teasingly. "Do it then. What judge in his right mind is going to give the father custody over the mother? If we go to court, you are just going to end up paying me more child support because I know you are making more money than you claim."

"Lena, I've tried to keep the courts out of this, but I'm not going to keep playing this game with you. I mean, come on! What's the deal with you? Are you jealous because I'm married now?"

She sucked her teeth again. "Jealous? Whatever. I'm getting off this phone now."

"Lena, if I don't see my daughter this weekend, I *will* be seeing you very soon in court."

"I look forward to it!"

I heard a click and immediately knew that she had hung up the phone. I let out an exhausted sigh and disconnected my end. No matter how much I tried to prepare myself for life, situations like this always seemed to come as a reminder that there was no such thing as having it all figured out. I tossed the phone onto the sofa and instinctually turned around, feeling a presence behind me. Amber stood at the entryway to the living room, watching me.

"Do we need to hire a lawyer? I know somebody."

I bet she did. Amber had an answer for everything. As much as I appreciated her help, some matters I just liked to handle for myself. "Maybe. I'll let you know."

"Mm," she replied, sounding unconvinced. "Dinner's ready." She looked me over suspiciously and then headed back into the kitchen.

I shook my head in defeat. Between Lena with her baby-momma drama, Jay with her overt flirting, and Amber with her raging pregnancy hormones, maybe I needed to enroll in this Husband 101 class after all. Or maybe I just needed to talk to someone I could depend on for good advice and hot meals that required more than just boiling water. Maybe I needed to talk to my mother, the one and only Ernestine Hayes, also known as Nessy.

Lesson 3: Know When It's Time To Leave & Cleave

Therefore a man shall leave his father and his mother and shall become untied and cleave to his wife, and they shall become one flesh.

(Genesis 2:24)

Three days later, I sat at the dining room table in my parents' home, debating whether I should go home and have Sunday dinner with my wife or stay and talk to my mother about the mounting weight on my shoulders. I know that it didn't seem like choosing between the two was a hard decision. The obvious choice is that I should have been with my wife, but I really needed to get my worries about taking Lena to court regarding Jonelle off my chest. Whenever I had a lot of stress in my life, my mother was always the one who knew how to put life into perspective for me.

"Where's your wife?" my brother Nelson asked me while licking barbeque sauce from my mother's famous babyback ribs off his left thumb. Although the question seemed harmless, I knew Nelson had an ulterior motive. Nelson Hayes was the oldest of the Hayes children and the only one who wasn't married. Nelson thought of himself as a playboy, a player, a lady's man, and every other word that equaled a refusal to settle down with one woman. He often projected his fear of commitment onto others, believing no man, except my father, should be married or in any type of monogamous relationship. He had not always been like this; an old college girlfriend who "dogged him out" was the one who ruined his perception of exclusivity, leaving every woman who followed to pay for her sins and every man who crossed Nelson's path to be warned about being tricked by the evil female species. I was no exception to the rule. Nelson had practically kidnapped me a day before my wedding, trying to break whatever love spell he was convinced that Amber had used to seduce me. Since the wedding, he continued to taunt me with unnecessary comments and questions, trying to prove to me that I had made a big mistake.

"She's at home. She wanted to attend to her own church this Sunday," I replied without looking up from my plate. I didn't want to see his face; I didn't want to see any of their faces. Around the table sat Nelson, my father, Dwayne, and my mother, Nessy. My sisters, Karyn and Cindy, were at home with their families where I was sure my father felt I needed to be as well. My father was a man who only talked when he was "in the mood." Sometimes he was stoic and would barely say anything for days. Other times, he was the life of the party, and we couldn't get him to stop yapping. When it came to personal matters, my dad often subscribed to the Bennett philosophy; his name was Bennett, and he wasn't in it. Unless a situation was completely out-of-control, Dwayne remained silent and kept his opinion to himself. Nonetheless, the look in his eyes spoke volumes about what he thought yet refused to say.

Nessy was the complete opposite. My momma spoke her mind freely and didn't pass up an opportunity to let her voice be heard, like at that very moment. "I don't know why you two go to different churches. A wife is supposed to follow her husband. She should be attending church with you. Hm. These young girls just don't know how to keep a man."

Before Amber and I got married, we thought the fact that we were both Christians was the only conversation that we needed to have about religion. We were wrong. I assumed that naturally Amber would start attending my church with me; however, I assumed wrong. Amber loved her church, and although she was willing to come to service with me once or twice a month, she wasn't interested in changing her membership. I, on the other hand, had been going to the same church my entire life. My father was a deacon there, my mother was a missionary, my uncle was the pastor; every person in my family had a role at that church, including me. I worked with the youth ministry from time-to-time. Despite the fact that I had been to Amber's church on several occasions and actually enjoyed it, there was no way that I could abandon the family church. It would have been equivalent to me turning my back on where I came from.

"That's why he should have never gotten married in the first place. Women always seem perfect at first, until they get what they want. Then their true colors come out," Nelson gloated.

I refrained from giving Nelson a malicious glare and instead forked pasta salad into my mouth. My mother's food was nothing short of heaven, but in the midst of my guilt and worries, the rich taste eluded me.

"Hush, Nelson," my mother intervened on my behalf. "Amber's a good woman. I like her; I *love* her. And I am glad that my baby settled down with someone who has got a good head on her shoulders. Now Eric, I know she got all that money and stuff, but she is going to have to remember that you are still the head of the home."

"Tell him, Momma. The head," Nelson interjected. "You're the man and she won't even come to church with you. Amber got you looking like a straight sucka."

"What, boy?" Nessy looked at Nelson as if he had completely lost his mind.

"Ma, Eric is a sucka, a wimp. Amber got him looking all soft! She runs things over there." Nelson shook his head in shame. "I never thought I would see the day when my baby brother would get his manhood snatched from him by some woman."

My father continued to suck on a rib bone as if the conversation was on mute, to him it probably was. My mother waved at Nelson as if she was magically waving his foolishness away. "Don't pay any attention to your brother. You know misery loves company."

I looked up at my mother and nodded. I had learned back in elementary school how to ignore my brother. He had always been overly confident and somewhat of a bully, constantly attempting to stir up my emotions. Early on, I tried to beat him by fighting back and arguing with him, but because he was bigger and cleverer than me, I could never win in an altercation with him. I quickly found out that because he was one of the most annoying people I knew, ignoring him was the best way to avoid conflict and beat him at his own game.

"I think I may have to file for custody against Lena," I finally said, confessing the real reason I was there and not with my wife.

My dad paused and blinked and then returned to enjoying his Sunday meal. Nelson chuckled and picked up his glass of cola, ending his laughter by slurping down the fizzy, dark brown liquid. My mom wiped her hands with a napkin and sat back in her chair.

"I've seen this coming for a while now," she began. "She doesn't want you to be happy because she's not happy, and she's gonna use that little girl to make sure she can control you. Well, baby, do what you have to do to be with your child."

I was about to respond back to my mother's statement when my cell phone began to vibrate. I pulled the phone out of my pocket and glanced at the screen. A picture of Amber and me during our honeymoon in Jamaica appeared on the display. Wanting to finish the conversation with my mom, I hit the ignore button. *Why did I do that?*

Two hours later when I walked into the front door of our home, Amber was sitting in the living room, waiting for me. I knew she was going to be livid. I had missed having Sunday dinner with her, and I had ignored her phone call. I had my reasons, but Amber wasn't going to see it my way. After years of being around her and almost a year of being married to her, I knew Amber would hit me with the old you-need-to-communicate-with-me lecture.

When I walked in the door, I was ready for her. She was flipping through a magazine and barely glanced up to roll her eyes at me. "So you don't know how to answer phones now?" she started.

I turned up the charm three notches, gave her my best baby-please-I-love-you look, and said, "Amber, I know, and I'm sorry. I just had some stuff on my mind that I needed to figure out. But listen, I've thought about it, and I'm going to take that Husband class you've been asking me about. Can you call the guy and tell him that I'm coming tomorrow?"

Amber scowled at me. I could tell that she wanted to stay angry with me, but I had said the words she had been begging for me to say for the last few months. In her mind, she had won, and to tell the truth, in my mind, she had won, too. With a huff, she stood up from the sofa and walked up to me, placing her hand on her hip and angling her head to the right. "I've already told him you were coming." She laughed and shook her head in amazement. "You think you're *so* slick. You thought you were just going to eat dinner at your momma's house, ignore my call, and then come in here with those puppy-dog eyes and say what you think I wanted to hear, and now everything is going to be all good again? I am your wife; I know you like the back of my hand. Well, momma's boy, there's a sink full of dishes with your name on them and don't even think that you'll be cuddling up with me tonight. You get *no* love." She took a moment to suck her teeth and roll her eyes again before walking away and disappearing up the stairs.

I must have forgotten whom I was married to. Amber Ross-Hayes was a woman like no other. I sighed deeply, cracked my knuckles, and unenthusiastically headed toward the kitchen to bust some suds.

Lesson 4: Sacrifice Is A Consequence Of Love

Husbands, love your wives, as Christ loved the church and gave
Himself up for her...Even so husbands should love their wives as
[being in a sense] their own bodies. He who loves his own wife loves
himself. For no man ever hated his own flesh, but nourishes and
carefully protects and cherishes it, as Christ does the church.

(Ephesians 5:25, 28-29)

The next day, I sat in the back of the choir room with eleven other men, wondering how Amber had duped me into taking this class and missing the first half of the Steelers versus Ravens game. It was as if she was psychic and knew that I was going to give her an excuse to force me to do what she wanted me to do. I had only been married for seven months and was thoroughly convinced about this women's intuition concept. There was no other way of explaining how women like Amber and my mother always stayed two steps ahead of men, especially me.

In the middle of my mental debate about the cunningness of women, a tall, middle-aged man entered the room and stood up front behind the wooden podium. The other men in the room quickly quieted their voices in expectation of what this man, whom I immediately assumed must be the teacher, would say.

"Good evening, brothers," he began. "For those of you who don't know me, my name is Minister Martin Woods, and I will be leading you through the Husband 101 course. You all can feel free to call me Martin. This is the second time we have taught this course, the first time being early last year. Many of those who took the Husband 101 and Wife 101 classes last year reported experiencing growth and positive changes in their marriages and romantic relationships. We wanted to offer the courses again a few months later, but due to other activities here at the church and our own conflicts of schedules, it has been about a year and a half since we have taught the last courses. However, now that we have worked out the kinks, we plan to start offering these classes more frequently.

"The purpose of Husband 101 is to help you better understand your role as a man, husband, and father. Of course, there is no way that in thirteen weeks we can cover the full essence of what it is to be a man, but we will at least begin working towards building a stronger foundation, helping you to understand who God intended you to be. With that being said, I am going to begin with a quick prayer, and then we will get into introductions."

We all bowed our heads at his cue, and he began to pray. "Almighty God, we thank You for this opportunity to edify one another. We ask for Your wisdom and understanding to fill our hearts and minds. Break down any and every barrier that stands between these men and Your plan for their lives. Let them leave this place better than they came, full of Your truth and grounded in Your Word. In Jesus' name, Amen."

"Amen," filled the room as we lifted our heads and waited for further instructions.

Martin moved from behind the podium and came closer to the group. "Now, we are going to go around the room and introduce ourselves. I want each of you to say your name, your marital status, and when or how you knew that your wife was the one you would marry. If you're not married, tell us how you think you will know when the time comes. I will begin.

"Like I said, my name is Martin Woods. I'm married and my wife, Lydia, teaches the Wife 101 class. I knew she was the one the first time I laid eyes on her twenty-three years ago. I met her at a Christmas party a mutual friend of ours was throwing. Y'all, she was *fiiinnneee!*" He laughed, and the rest of us joined in.

"But when I approached her, she wasn't trying to hear it. I think that's what did it for me, the fact that she wasn't like the other women. I mean she really played hard to get, and you all know that we men like a bit of a challenge. At the time, other women were happy as long as a man looked good, had a car, and a few bucks in his pocket, but not Lydia. No, she made me, as the young people say, 'step up my game.' I practically had to stalk that woman to get her to go out on a date with me, but chasing her was worth it. We got married a year later on New Year's Eve. In a few months, we will be celebrating our 22nd Anniversary." He sighed. "God is good."

He pointed at a young man near the front of the room, signaling him to give his introduction. A minute later, I had learned that his name was Kevin, he was twenty-eight, was recently engaged to a woman named Rochelle, and believed she was the one because she had caused him to give up causal dating and make a serious commitment. Ten minutes later, it was my turn to speak.

"My name is Eric Hayes. My wife's name is Amber, and we're still in our first year of marriage. How did I know she was the one? Uh, I used to work for her, and one day she asked me to go out of town with her for this business event. To make a long story short, she needed me to stand up for her, to be there for her. I had always viewed her as this strong woman who didn't need anyone, but at that moment, I realized how vulnerable she really was, and I wanted to be the one who she could lean on."

The men in the room nodded their heads as if they understood where I was coming from.

"So you're Eric," Martin said with a grin. I could only imagine what Amber had told him about me. "Nice to finally meet you."

I nodded in response, and Martin shifted his focus from me and returned to addressing the class. "During this course, we are going to study what love is. People say the word 'love' all of the time, but have no clue what it really means to love someone. What is love? How do you know that you love someone? What is the difference between love and lust? If we want to be good husbands, good fathers, good men, we have to reflect who God is, and He is love."

Martin picked up a stack of papers from the podium and began distributing them to the class. "Now, fellas, I need for you all to come to this class ready to be honest about yourselves, your women, and your relationship with God. We are going to talk about some real stuff in here, and some secrets may come out, some regrets may come out, but that's good! We cannot be free to be the men we are supposed to be until we become free of all of the burdens that hold us back in our loving. Right now, I'm passing out a confidentiality agreement. I know it might sound crazy, but we need to establish this group as a circle of trust. Like Vegas, whatever is said in here, stays in here. We cannot afford for anyone not to be honest or to hold back because he is afraid what he says is going to get back to his wife or the church. Now, of course, if the matter is life threatening or something like that, we will have to deal with it appropriately. I want you to take a few minutes, read over the agreement, and if you intend to continue on in the class, sign it and pass it back up to the front."

We all took a few minutes to follow Martin's directives, submitting the forms back to him. Martin collected them and stuffed them into a folder. He then opened a maroon colored Bible that rested atop of the podium.

"This course will focus on the comprehension and application of the chapter in the Bible that defines love, I Corinthians 13, but before we dive into Corinthians, we are going to spend the rest of our time today discussing Ephesians 5:21-33. Please take out your Bibles and turn to these verses. I will read them out loud using the Amplified version of the Bible."

The sound of shuffling and pages turning filled the room. When the noise quieted, Martin began to read out loud. "Starting at verse twenty-one. 'Be subject to one another out of reverence for Christ, the Messiah, the Anointed One. Wives, be subject, be submissive and adapt yourselves to your own husbands as a service to the Lord. For the husband is the head of the wife as Christ is the Head of the church, Himself the Savior of His body. As the church is subject to Christ, so let wives also be subject in everything to their husbands. Husbands, love your wives, as Christ loved the church and gave Himself up for her, so that He might sanctify her, having cleansed her by the washing of water with the Word, that He might present the church to Himself in glorious splendor, without spot or wrinkle or any such things, that she might be holy and faultless. Even so husbands should love their wives as being in a sense their own bodies. He who loves his own wife loves himself. For no man ever hated his own flesh, but nourishes and carefully protects and cherishes it, as Christ does the church, because we are members, parts, of His body. For this reason, a man shall leave his father and his mother and shall be joined to his wife, and the two shall become one flesh. This mystery is very great, but I speak concerning the relation of Christ and the church. However, let each man of you, without exception, love his wife as being in a sense his very own self; and let the wife see that she respects and reverences her husband, that she notices him, regards him, honors him, prefers him, venerates, and esteems him; and that she defers to him, praises him, and loves and admires him exceedingly.' "

He scanned the room and chuckled. "I am going to admit, fellas, I was a little unsure of what to teach you all or even how I could help you all become better men. When my wife and I took on this endeavor, she instantly knew that God was leading her to study and share Proverbs 31 with her class. Me, on the other hand, the Bible verses weren't so clear. I considered many different approaches to this course, and at one point really thought I had something from the Old Testament that would work. I began studying and writing notes and was prepared to move forward in a certain direction. However, one morning, as I lay in my bed, God directed me to teach about love. I was a little hesitant because Lydia and I had already agreed to use the passage on love from Corinthians for our combined gender class, but I just couldn't shake the pull in my spirit to focus on the topic of love. So I talked to my wife again, and we agreed to change our plans for the combined class and for me to use the infamous definition of love in the Husband 101 class. I am giving you this background information for a reason.

"Sometimes as men, we think we've got it all figured out. We think we know what we're doing, what God would have us to do. We've got a plan, we're working our plan, and we are so sure that our plan is what we have to do, what we need to do. Then God speaks to us and says, 'No, take a different path. Go a different way. This is not the way.' And what do we do? We fight it. We resist. We can't let go of our plans. We have worked too hard, strategized too much, gotten so caught up in our determination to make it work that we are unwilling to heed to God's voice. So we continue on down the wrong path. Our pride won't let us turn back. And one day, we wake up, and our whole lives are in shambles."

As he spoke, he began to pace back and forth across the front of the room. "Gentlemen, we have to let God leads us in all that we do. It cannot be our way; it has to be His way. Some of you in this room right now are trying to do it your way. You think that you are heading down the path that will bring you to where you want to be. During this class, you will be challenged to take a different path, the path of love. Most of us really have no idea what love is all about. We toss the word around like it's a basketball, and we're playing a pick-up game of two-on-two. But truly understanding and embracing love, the way God intended, will change your decisions, your dating, your marriages, your path; it will change you."

He stopped walking and picked up his Bible. "Before we get into studying the definition of love, we must first examine the Bible's directive to men about love. Most of you have probably read or heard of these verses in the fifth chapter of Ephesians. We especially love the part about wives submitting themselves to their husbands, don't we?"

Several of the men in the room laughed and bobbed their heads in agreement.

"But the part that we as men really need to pay attention to is what comes before and after. The verse prior says to be subject to each other out of respect for Christ. How many men will throw in their wives faces that the Bible says you're supposed to submit to me, yet they are not in return submitting themselves to their wives or God? Verse twenty-one states that we are all to be subject, to be accountable, to be liable, to follow, to support one another. This is not a one-sided deal. Every good leader knows that to be the best leader, you must also know when to follow. Yes, you are the head, but that does not mean you should not allow your wife to lead sometimes. Some things she is just better at than you, and it's not always cooking and cleaning. She may be better at managing finances, better with negotiating with others, or better at coming up with new ideas. It does not take anything away from you to step back and say, 'Baby, I know that you are really good at doing this, so I'm going to let you handle it or decide how we should handle it.' Making a statement like that and following through does not reduce you as a man or the head in any manner at all. Actually, it makes you a stronger and more secure man to be able to admit her strengths and your weaknesses."

A few men grunted in approval while many of us remained quiet. I understood what he was saying. Amber was a much better manager of finances than I was. She knew how to organize, juggle, and keep things afloat in a way that amazed me. I didn't have a problem with her writing out the checks to pay the bills. In all honesty, she made way more money than I did, and some of her expenses from prior to our marriage, I didn't want to touch with a ten-foot pole. When we got married, we agreed to move into her house because I was renting a two-bedroom apartment at the time. Although she had bought the house for almost half of its value and with a hefty down payment, she was in a 15-year mortgage and paying double the amount every month to have it paid off in less than seven years. She had added my name to the deed and the mortgage, but technically, I wasn't contributing to the house payments. What was left of my income after taxes and child support went toward other household bills and car payments. I was grateful to Amber for carrying the load the way she did and still allowing me to live like a king, but deep inside I couldn't shake the feeling of wishing I had more money to bring to the table. Getting commercial clients like Jay was important to me because it meant I could offer more to my household and stop feeling as if I were living off of my financially secure wife.

As various thoughts swirled through my mind, I attempted to focus my attention back on Martin's lesson. "The verses following go on to state that a man is to love his wife like Christ loved the church and gave His life for it. Love equals sacrifice. Let me say it another way. Sacrifice is a consequence of love. You cannot truly love someone, anyone, if you are not willing to sacrifice something for her. It cannot always be your way. You have to be able to give up something that is important to you. Love is demonstrative, and the demonstration of love is sacrifice. Christ loved us so much that He gave up His life so that we could live.

"What has always struck me about these verses is the fact that women are directed to submit themselves, to honor and to respect their husbands. It takes three and a half verses to explain this concept to women, but when men are instructed to love their wives, it takes eight and a half verses to explain this concept to men. Doesn't that seem unusual to any of you? Women aren't told to love their husbands, and the writer takes less than four verses to get the point across to them of what they are supposed to do. Why do you think this is? Well, here is my theory.

"First, women don't have to be told to love their husbands because for the most part, they already do. A woman has an innate ability to love people in a way that a man cannot understand. A woman will meet a man one time and be head over hills, ready to get married. Most of us men may like a woman when we meet her, but it will probably take some time to develop real emotions for her. Women forgive easier, connect quicker, and feel stronger than men feel. A man could beat a woman down, call her every name under the sun except a child of God, and almost kill her, and that woman, although she may be hurt may still say, 'I still love him.' For men, loving seems more complicated, and the author of Ephesians, the Apostle Paul, understands that it is going to take a little extra effort to explain this idea of 'loving their wives' to men."

I was starting to like Martin. He was a straight to the point, no nonsense kind of guy. Who couldn't respect that in a man?

Martin put down his bible on the podium and picked up another stack of papers. "We are going to come back to these verses at the end of our thirteen weeks. Hopefully, by that time, you all will have a better understanding of love, which will make these verses even more profound for you. Before we leave tonight, I am going to have you do one quick exercise." Martin began handing out the new, mostly blank sheets of paper. "I am passing out a piece of paper that has one question on it: Why do I love my wife? If you are not married, you can change the word to girlfriend or fiancé. If you're not in a relationship, think about the last serious relationship you had with someone that you loved. Take a few moments and write down your answer. I am going to collect your answers, seal them up in this envelope, and we will return to your answers toward the end of our thirteen weeks."

We completed the exercise, turned our papers in, and ended the lesson with a prayer. On my way home, I thought about my answer to the exercise's question. "I love my wife because when I'm with her I feel complete. She is everything that I'm not." I wasn't sure if it was the answer Martin was looking for, but it was an honest answer. Before my relationship with Amber, so much of my life felt lacking, like there was something missing that I just couldn't seem to work out for myself. With Amber by my side, I now felt invincible, like there was nothing that we couldn't achieve together. The thought caused me to smile, and I wore that smile all the way home.

"Hey baby," Amber greeted me when I entered our bedroom that evening.

"Hey you," I responded as I quickly kissed her and proceeded to change into a pair of sweatpants and a T-shirt. The game was now in the third quarter, and if I changed quickly enough and made a couple sandwiches, I could at least catch the full fourth quarter.

"How was the class?" she asked as she turned her attention away from the novel she was reading and looked up at me.

"It's was good. Martin seems decent," I said coolly, trying not to get into a long conversation with her about it. I knew Amber wanted all the details, but I wanted to watch football.

"Oh-kay," she replied, catching on to my I-don't-want-to-talk-about-it-now vibe. "Oh yeah. You ran out of here so fast this evening that you left your cell phone on the counter. I plugged it up to save the battery. It's over there on the dresser."

I halted midway through sliding my feet into a clean pair of socks. *I left my phone here?* Shrugging at the idea, I finished putting on my socks and stood up.

"It rang a few times, but I didn't answer it. The caller-ID said it was someone named Jay. You might want to call him back before it gets too late," she said casually.

My eyes grew as big as saucers, but my back was turned toward her so she didn't see my momentary panic. I quickly calmed myself, grabbed my cell phone off the dresser, mumbled "thanks" to her, and left the room.

Lesson 5: Be Able To Recognize The Signs

A wise man suspects danger and cautiously avoids evil, but the fool
bears himself insolently and [presumptuously] confident.

(Proverbs 14:16)

I didn't call Jay back that night. It was getting late, and I thought it
would be inappropriate. Not only that, but I couldn't risk being on the
phone with her (even if it was just business) and having Amber sneak
up on me, asking questions. I believed in women's intuition way too
much to take that chance. It wasn't until eleven o'clock the next
morning when I was finally able to return Jay's call.

"Sorry it's taken me a bit to get back to you. I left my phone at
home yesterday," I explained.

"No problem, Eric. I understand you're a busy and important
man," Jay replied gently.

I stifled a chuckle. This woman certainly knew how to be
charming. "Well, thanks for understanding. What can I do for you?"

"I'm glad you asked. I recently got the inside scoop on a building
in Little Five Points. I heard it's about to go into foreclosure so the
owner is trying to get rid of it quickly. If I text you the address, can you
look into it for me? Maybe we can even go check it out today?" she
asked, full of hope. "Or am I expecting too much, too soon? I know its
last minute, and you have other things to do."

Yes, I had other things to do, but she was ready to buy, so I
couldn't turn her down. "No, I'll look into it. Send me the address

now, and I will get on the horn and see what I can do. I'll call you back and let you know."

"Thanks, Eric! You're the best!" she squealed.

To me, it was obvious that Jay was a master at saying the right words to get what she wanted. I had dated women like her before; Lena to name one. Trickery was one of the reasons Lena and I never worked out. She constantly attempted to manipulate me using her words, and although her antics were somewhat "cute" at the beginning, eventually they became tiresome. If Jay were anything like Lena, I would need to proceed with caution. I made a mental note to be careful of how I allowed Jay's words to affect me. With yellow caution flags circling my thoughts, I hung up the phone, sighed heavily, and got to work on her request.

Five o'clock in Atlanta was rush hour. It was also the time Jay and I were scheduled to meet with Walter Parke, the owner of the commercial property in Little Five Points. Thinking about my conflicting impressions about Jay, I pulled in front of the building. On one hand, she was a wealthy client who was entrusting my company to help her locate and attain another site for her business. Selling real estate to the owner of Hotlanta Fitness was a lucrative opportunity, something I wanted and needed badly. However, on the other hand, she was way too flirtatious and seemed to have an agenda when it came to me. I wasn't naive to the woman's tactics—most men wouldn't be—but going along with her flirtation for the sake of financial and career payout felt worth it. I had been working my whole life to "make a dollar out of fifteen cents." Finally, I was living comfortably, but I was doing so on the generosity and achievements of my wife. As a man, I craved my own sense of accomplishment. I didn't want to be known as the type of man whose success was based on marrying a woman of status. I had to blaze my own path, create my own accolades.

I was grateful that Amber had offered me her real estate business. Before she did, I was worried sick about finding employment once we married. By me working for her realty, we knew our changing relationship would negatively impact the business and our home front. I was certain that I couldn't be the head of the household at night while submitting to her authority during the workday, and she knew she couldn't handle the shifts in roles either. Naturally, I planned to leave the realty and find a job elsewhere, but instead, Amber gave me majority ownership of the company so that I wouldn't have to quit and start over.

Yes, she had two other businesses to keep her occupied, but the realty was her first venture and her baby. Giving it to me had to have been a tough and emotional decision for her. Her support and selflessness made me love her even more. I mean, how many women would make that kind of sacrifice for her man? Amber announced her decision to hand the business over to me during our wedding which wasn't the most humble approach, but I understood her motivation wasn't to be showy, but to share that moment with our closest friends and family. So, I brushed off the slight embarrassment at the time and accepted her well-intentioned gift.

Nevertheless, in the back of my mind, Amber's generosity still felt like a handout, something I had not worked for and didn't earn. In order to feel deserving, I had to somehow make the business my own, make it something I could claim the rights to. By formulating commercial deals, like the one I was working on with Jay, I believed that I would feel more at ease in my position as both CEO and head-of-household. As I said, I needed this opportunity with Jay, and although she was like fire, I was hoping and praying that playing with her wouldn't leave me burned.

I turned off the engine to my Cadillac CTS-V Sedan (a birthday gift from my loving wife), and got out of the car, searching the parking lot for Mr. Parke or Jay. Before I could close my car door, a lipstick red Mercedes Benz SLS AMG Coupe pulled up next to me. Jay waved from inside the car and then hit a button, causing the car's passenger side gullwing door to raise and open.

She pushed her sunglasses down over her nose to reveal her dark chestnut eyes and extended eyelashes. "Eric! Is the guy here yet?"

I raised my hands as if to say I wasn't sure. "I don't see anyone."

"Well, get in. We can wait in my car until he shows up."

Getting inside her car may not have been the smartest move I've ever made, but I was dying to experience the vehicle's sleekness and luxury. She must have paid a boatload of cash because it was at minimum a $200K car, plus she had everything customized. I was truly in awe. Excitedly, I locked my car using its remote and slid into the passenger seat of her vehicle, my nostrils instantly being assaulted by that new car smell. "Nice ride," I said, trying not to sound too impressed. She hit the button again causing the door on my side to close. I was in love . . . with the car.

Jay ran the tips of her pink painted, acrylic nails over the steering wheel. "Thanks. I just got it over the summer. I usually have my driver chauffeur me in the Maybach, but when I just want to be free and drive myself, I take this baby out." After spending a moment gazing proudly at her dashboard, she nodded in the direction of my Caddy. "Your car isn't too shabby, either. Looks new."

I looked over at my car. Before that moment, I had been thrilled about my shiny new ride. I had never had a brand new vehicle, much less a Cadillac. I was surprised when Amber called me on my birthday and told me that her Escalade had broken down, that she was at the dealership getting it fixed, and desperately needed me to come pick her up. The SUV was less than three years old and still under warranty so I couldn't imagine what was wrong with it. When I parked my Chevy Impala in front of the dealership, Amber rushed out of the building and immediately demanded my keys. Confused, I passed her the keys, thinking she just wanted to drive home. Instead, she tossed me the keys to the Cadillac CTS that was parked two cars down and said, "I'll drive your old car home, so that you can take your new one for a spin." I was floored, but then again, Amber was always full of surprises. I had been driving the Cadillac ever since, like it was a golden goose, ignoring my tarp-covered Impala in the driveway as if it was a bill collector. Until that very moment, my Caddy was a slice of heaven, but sitting in Jay's Benz made my heavenly car look like a rusty hooptie.

I shook the covetous thoughts out my head and reminded myself how blessed I was. "It is. My wife bought it for me back in March." There it was. I said it: I'm married. In case she hadn't noticed the platinum and diamond band on my left ring finger, my statement should have resolved any confusion between us.

"Well, that was nice of her. I see she has good taste," she said as if she was completely unfazed by my announcement. "I almost got married once, but he just wasn't the right guy for me. Plus, I didn't fully trust him, and you gotta have trust to have a good marriage, right?"

"Right."

She flashed a confident smile. "You seem trustworthy; it's understandable that you're married. How long have you been hitched?"

"Seven months." I felt a little weird discussing my marriage with her, but it was just small talk so I figured it couldn't hurt.

"Seven months? You're still newlyweds?"

"I guess you can say that."

She removed the sunglasses completely from her face and made eye contact with me. "Be honest with me. Is marriage really what you thought it would be?"

From talking to others, I knew that marriage was never what you thought it was going to be, but I didn't regret my decision to take the plunge. "Mostly. It has its good and bad moments like everything in life, but I found someone that I love, and it was time for me to move forward with my life. I never dreamed I would have ended up with someone like her. She's very special."

She tilted her head in interest. "Awe, that's sweet. She sounds really nice. What does she do? Is she like a teacher or something?"

I leaned back against the leather seats; they felt amazingly cozy. This car was so cool! "No. She's a business owner. She actually used to be the CEO of the realty."

Her eyebrows arched higher in surprise. "Oh, so she's the Ross in Hayes and Ross?"

"Yeah. That's her," I admitted smugly. I could tell that she thought I was married to an average woman. She had no clue. Amber could stand up toe-to-toe against her on any day.

"Wow. Maybe one day I'll have the pleasure of meeting her." She looked up into the rearview mirror and smiled. "Is that the guy pulling up behind us? I think so. Let's get moving." She hit another button and this time, both doors flew up and open. I slowly crawled out of her Benz, trying to take the sumptuous experience with me. *Man,* I thought. *When I get this company making big bucks, I'm trading in the Caddy and buying me a Benz, fully loaded!*

My meeting with Jay and Mr. Parke had gone pretty well, and she was considering the property. It was a prime location, had more than ample space for a gym, and the price had been dropped significantly. Honestly, I believed she would buy it, but she first wanted to explore a few other options. In talking to Mr. Parke, we learned that the property was in pre-foreclosure status. This status meant we didn't have a large window of time to make an offer to the bank, but we didn't have to move immediately either. We probably could look around for another 30 days or so before making our offer. He had some connections within the bank that held the mortgage and they had agreed to give him a little extra time to sell the property.

On Friday, I took the day off of work to go to Amber's prenatal check-up. I wasn't too crazy about being at the doctor's office and watching this male doctor "touch" my wife, but it was all a part of the baby process. I had gone through it all with Lena, and once again, I would have to suck it up and get through it with Amber.

After the examination, Amber removed the paper gown and attempted to get dressed quickly before the doctor returned. With pleasure, I watched her scurry around the room, half clothed, trying to slip on a pair of jeans without letting her bare feet touch the floor. Amber was obsessed with avoiding getting athlete's foot from walking on public floors without shoes. She cringed at the thought of going through security at the airport because of the requirement to remove her shoes. Even now, with us being in a healthcare setting that should have been a mostly clean environment, she was taking no chances. She carefully stepped on top of her shoes while trying to balance herself and insert each foot into the pant leg. It wasn't working. I let out a short laugh when she lost her balance and fell over onto the examination bed.

"Stop laughing and come over here and help me!" she demanded.

I shook my head at my adorable, bossy wife. No one else but Amber could make a routine doctor's visit entertaining. I got up from my seat in the corner and walked over to her, allowing her to lean against me as she slid on her jeans. By the time she pulled her cream-colored, cotton sweater over her head, the doctor was knocking on the door. Amber sat on the edge of the table, putting on her shoes as Dr. Keaton flipped through her chart for a second before pulling up another chair and sitting down to begin our consultation.

"Mrs. Hayes, your blood pressure is still elevated and still poses a risk to both you and your baby. Have you been relaxing like we discussed?" he asked.

Amber glanced at me as if she were caught with her hand in the cookie jar. "I'm trying to, Dr. Keaton. I just have a lot of responsibilities, and it is really hard for me to just stop my life right now."

He rested the paperwork on a nearby countertop and looked at Amber with gentle eyes. "I understand that you're a busy woman, Mrs. Hayes. However, it's my job as your physician to keep you healthy. I am very concerned about this pregnancy. It is my recommendation that you take a leave of absence from work."

An expression of terror spread over Amber's face as if he had just notified her that the government was banning fried chicken. "But a lot of women have high blood pressure and have healthy babies all the time. Why am I any different?"

"You are already complaining of headaches which are a common symptom of preeclampsia. Now, I don't think you are at that level of risk yet, but if you don't slow down, it could get there. I want you to start exercising, but nothing too strenuous, something like walking. Of course, reduce your salt intake, and stay away from work. I'm sure you have employees that can step up and handle things while you take care of yourself."

I supportively rubbed her back. "Amber, baby, he's only trying to help us."

She blew out a frustrated sigh. "I know. I know. Thanks, Dr. Keaton. I'll . . . back up from work."

He smiled politely, shook our hands, and left the room. I gazed at my wife in sympathy and sorrow. I knew that Amber could not refrain from working; it wasn't in her genes. Although she was a good woman and had made many efforts to prioritize her family, completely letting go of her career aspirations was a challenge for her. For the time being, I guess that made two of us.

Lesson 6: Everything Means Nothing Without Love

And if I have prophetic powers (the gift of interpreting the divine will and purpose), and understand all the secret truths and mysteries and possess all knowledge, and if I have [sufficient] faith so that I can remove mountains, but have not love (God's love in me) I am nothing.

(I Corinthians 13:2)

"Welcome back, brothers. I am glad to see that all of you have returned and that I didn't scare anyone off last week," Minster Martin said at the beginning of our second class.

After Amber's doctor's appointment on Friday, I was motivated to take care of a few overlooked family-related needs. I figured if she saw me doing more around the house, it would help her to feel more comfortable stepping back and letting someone else have control (at least while she was pregnant). On Saturday, I hand washed the Escalade, the CTS, and the Mustang (her other car) and changed the oil in all of them. I raked the lawn and bagged up the fallen leaves. I changed the batteries in the smoke detectors and replaced a few blown out light bulbs. I even took her out to dinner at the Cheesecake Factory at Perimeter Mall, which was one of her favorite spots. On Sunday, I visited her church with her and helped make Sunday dinner. I was so much on a roll that on Monday morning, instead of going straight to the office, I made her breakfast-in-bed and then went down to the courthouse to file for joint custody of Jonelle. I knew that Lena was going to hit the roof when she received the court date, but I had to be a man and stand up to her. I deserved the right to see my daughter on a consistent basis, not just when Lena felt like being nice. I was done with arguing with her about the issue. At this point, I was ready to let the courts work it out. By the time I got to class that evening, I was feeling exhausted, but proud of myself.

The sound of Martin's authoritative voice filled the room. "Let's recap on what we've discussed so far. We started our time together examining Ephesians chapter five as it relates to what a man is instructed to do for his wife; he is directed to love her. This love for her is compared to Christ's love for us, the church. So as Christ loved the church in a sacrificial manner that He gave Himself, His life for us, now we as men are expected to love our wives as such that we sacrifice ourselves for them. Now, there is so much to say about sacrifice as a component of love, and we will come back to this idea repeatedly during the course. So, let's begin by attempting to truly understand this word love. What does it mean? Why is it so important? How does one four-letter-word lead to God coming down in the flesh and giving up Himself for us?"

He picked up his Bible and the rest of us followed his lead.

"Let's all turn to I Corinthians 13. We are going to focus today on verses 1-3. I am again reading from the Amplified version." He gave us a moment to get to the page before continuing. "It reads, 'If I can speak in the tongues of men and even of angels, but have not love, that reasoning, intentional, spiritual devotion such as inspired by God's love for and in us, I am only a noisy gong or a clanging cymbal. And if I have prophetic powers, the gift of interpreting the divine will and purpose, and understand all the secret truths and mysteries and possess all knowledge, and if I have sufficient faith so that I can remove mountains, but have not love, God's love in me, I am nothing. Even if I dole out all that I have to the poor in providing food, and if I surrender my body to be burned or in order that I may glory, but have not love, God's love in me, I gain nothing.' Um hm. Let me repeat that: I am only, I am nothing, I gain nothing."

Although I was familiar with those three verses, I waited in expectation for Martin to break them down in a way I hadn't considered. He did not disappoint me.

"Corinthians, like Ephesians, is written by the Apostle Paul as letters to the church at Corinth, responding to problems and tensions within the church. In these first three verses of the thirteenth chapter of this first book of Corinthians, three conclusions are made: Without love I am only, I am nothing, I gain nothing."

He laid his Bible down on the podium and began to walk around the room as he talked. "Verse one concentrates on the ability to speak. In our society we love people who speak well. From preachers to politicians, if you can use big words and say things in an eloquent way and have deep conversations, we will flock to you. I mean honestly, who wants a leader with a speech impediment like a lisp or a stutter? Who wants to have a discussion with people who cannot clearly communicate their views? Who wants to be forced to listen to a lecture by someone who uses a bunch of slang or cannot articulate his or her words? No one. Paul expands the idea and says, even if I can speak every language better than any man out there, or even if I can speak like the angels, without love, God's love, I am just making noise. Some of you may be just noise makers in your home. You are talking, saying all the right things, but because of the absence of God's love, it all sounds like Charlie Brown's teacher. 'Wan-wan-wan wan-wan.' Your words fall on deaf ears. You're wondering why no one listens when you speak, why no one follows your directions, why no one seems to care what you have to say. Your words are just noise. The love is missing."

He moved back over to the podium and glanced down at the Bible before saying, "The second verse says that you can have all the knowledge in the world, all the wisdom, just know everything. You could be considered the smartest man on earth. You could be able to answer questions, like where is Jimmy Hoffa and who killed the Notorious BIG? But without love, you are nothing. Intelligence minus love might be the problem for some of you. You might be a brilliant person, see and understand things that no one else does, but you can't figure out why no one gives you any credit, why no one promotes you, why no one even likes you. You're intelligent, you're wise, but without love, you're nothing.

"Finally, the third verse says that even if you gave everything you have, every dime you have, every minute of your time, even your body or life up for others, if you do not have love, God's love, you have gained nothing from all of your sacrifices. I mean you could be the most generous philanthropist alive or you could practically live at the soup kitchen. You could be like Joan of Arc, burning at the stake for your cause, but if love is not in you, you have profited nothing from all of your efforts. Love, it takes love, and this might be your issue. You give and you give. You try to buy people with gifts. You think that if you give all of your time or sacrifice your safety that people will respect you, adore you. You will spend every dollar you make trying to wine and dine your wife. She has all of the newest and most expensive jewelry, lavish cars and houses, everything she could ever want, but your love because God's love is not in you. To her, you've done nothing at all. She still wants a divorce, and she still doesn't appreciate or respect you. On her way out the door she tells you, 'Get your checkbook ready, Mister. I want half.' "

A couple of brothers in the class let out laughs at the last statement. I figured we all knew men who thought they could buy people, men like Jonathan Gold. Gold was a former business associate of Amber's and her fiancé for all of a month. I became angry every time I thought about his smug face. Amber and I had been hanging out, trying to get to know each other, but what I didn't know was that she was also going out on dates with Gold. He proposed to her, and she got caught up in the moment and said yes. I found out a couple of weeks later and was heartbroken. I quit my job at the realty and everything!

To make a long story short, she dumped him and her business deal with his company and came running back to me once she realized that she didn't love him, that she really loved me. Since then, he'd called a few times and shown up at a few functions. Whenever I saw him, I'd pull Amber a little closer to remind him that all of his money and ego couldn't out beat a godly man when it came to a virtuous woman in training (what Amber likes to call herself). He thought he could buy her heart, but he didn't realize although some people come with a price tag, hearts never do. Reminiscing on the matter, I smiled to myself. Comparing Martin's words to Jonathan Gold helped me to understand the scripture even better.

Martin counted to three on his fingers. "Words, thoughts, and actions. Everything we do in this world revolves around what we say or communicate, how we think and feel, and what we do or how we behave. Paul is revealing to us that our words, thoughts, and actions, how we live means absolutely nothing in the end if love is not in the midst of motivation. God is love, and love is God, so basically we can replace the word love and say that none of our communication, none of our knowledge, and nothing that we do even matters if God is not in it.

"I'm going to give you all another assignment. Take out your notebooks and pens if you don't already have them out. On a sheet of paper, I want you to write down the things that you are most proud of. Write down your accomplishments, your hopes, and dreams. What is it that you are working towards? What is it that you are really good at? What's your talent or skill? Take a few minutes to write a list of these things."

We all followed his directives and began writing out our lists. I jotted down that I was most proud of my daughter, my marriage, my career, and being a Christian. My accomplishments included graduating from high school, attending college (although I didn't finish), and getting my real estate and brokers licenses. My hopes and dreams were eventually to return to school and finish my degree, to build a successful business that would allow me to provide for my family and leave behind an inheritance for my children, and to see my kids grow up to be healthy and productive adults. I was working towards developing my marriage and my new company, as well as getting custody of my child. I was really good at coming up with new ideas, talking to people, working with computers, selling products, and managing others. I finished my list just in time to hear Martin's next instructions.

"Now, tear the piece of paper out of your notebook and take another piece of paper from your notebook, leave it in the notebook, but copy the list you have onto that new piece of paper."

We all complied, tearing our lists out of our notebooks and copying them onto another sheet.

"Okay, the piece of paper that you have torn out, I want you to rip it up. Tear it into pieces and come up to the front and throw the pieces away into the trash can up here."

Everyone in the room halted for a few seconds, surprised by Martin's command. We had taken the time to write this special list and now he wanted us to destroy it? We all looked at each other with clueless expressions and then hesitantly ripped up our first lists and discarded them into the garbage.

When the last man returned to his seat, Martin smiled at us and said, "The next thing I want you to do is take the remaining list and in big letters covering the entire page, write the letters L-O-V-E."

As Martin instructed, I wrote the word LOVE in big letters across my second list, preparing myself to have to destroy this one as well.

Martin stood before us, seeming to sense our anxieties about our second lists. "I know it had to hurt some of you when you had to rip up the paper with the things that were important to you, but that's what happens without love. Your plans, hopes, and dreams are nothing. All that you think matters, doesn't. But when you covered what was important with love, now your plans, hopes, and dreams are something. Now they matter. Now they remain."

Martin's words cut deep, and I thought about them for the rest of the evening. Was God's love a part of everything that was important to me? If not, were all of my efforts really useless? Was it in the Spirit of

Love that I was seeking custody of Jonelle? Was love involved in my plans to build the realty? Was God's love at the center of all of my plans, hopes, and dreams? If it wasn't, I sure wanted it to be. I decided that night that I would make sure that love covered all of my decisions from that moment on. Too bad for me that life makes you forget yesterday's promises.

Lesson 7: When It Sounds Too Good To Be True . . .

The simpleton believes every word he hears, but the prudent man looks and considers well where he is going. (Proverbs 14:15)

A few evenings later, Amber and I cuddled on the living room sofa, watching one of her favorite movies, *Love Jones*, and arguing over whether or not Darius Lovehall was wrong for having his old fling Lisa Martin's phone number on the wall where his girlfriend, Nina Mosley, could see it.

"You know he was dead wrong!" Amber shouted, pulling away from me as if I had the cooties. "Of course, she was going to be insecure. What woman or man likes having someone else thrown up in their face like that?"

"True. But he told her that nothing was going on between them so she just should have believed him, especially after she went back to her ex-fiancé and was hanging out with his friend Wood," I contested.

"Now you know it wasn't even like that between her and Wood. And the ex? Okay, she was dirty for that, but that was water under the bridge, so he can't even bring that back up," she rationalized.

We stared at each other for a few seconds, mulling over her last statement, and then both burst into laughter.

"Come on, baby," I chuckled. "You know what you said doesn't even make sense! You just don't want to admit that I'm right."

"That's because you're wrong. You're always–"

Her words were cut short by the sound of the doorbell ringing and knocking at our front door. We looked at each other quizzically, wondering who was beating on our door as if they were the police. Whoever it was, they obviously disagreed with the adage, "Patience is a virtue."

Amber stood up and allowed me to get off the sofa to answer the door. The door didn't have a peephole, so I was forced to open it blindly and face whoever had lost his or her mind. I swung the door open with a grudge, prepared to let the caller have a verbal beat down.

It was Lena.

She stood on the porch's landing, her short stature puffed up as if she was 6-feet tall instead of 5'2. The moment she saw me, she glared at me with enough anger to burn down Sodom and Gomorrah. "You've got some nerve!" she screamed at me and pushed pass me into the foyer. "Of all the low down, dirty tricks you could pull! I can't believe you, Eric!"

By this time, Amber had made her way into the foyer and was leaning against the wall with her arms crossed, mentally daring Lena to test her. "What's going on, Eric?" she asked calmly, but I knew Amber. She was gearing up for a fight.

I figured Lena must have received the court papers; it was the only explanation for why she was "cutting a fool." She never came to our house, not even to drop off Jonelle. She expected me to come to her, and I only complied to keep her from having another excuse to withhold my child from me.

"I'm not sure yet. Lena hasn't said why she's here," I responded, waiting for Lena to spill the beans and say why she was so upset.

Lena rolled her eyes. "You know why I'm here; don't play stupid Eric! I'm pretty sure your woman knows, too!"

Amber took a step forward, but I raised my hand and signaled her to remain where she was.

I decided to fess up. "I'm assuming that you got the papers with the court date. Am I right?"

"Yeah, I got those ridiculous papers. You think you're going to just take my daughter away from me? You are sorely mistaken!" She waved her index finger at me as if I was a little boy.

I huffed. "Lena, I'm not trying to take Jonelle away from you. I just want joint custody. I deserve to be able to spend just as much time with her as you do without you always trying to control everything."

"You don't deserve anything! Where were you all these years while I've been raising her alone? I was the one who made sure she ate every day, clothed her, got her ready for school, me! Now all of a sudden, you marry Miss Thing over there, and you wanna play daddy? Not with my child, you won't!"

Amber took another step forward. "Did she just call me Miss Thing?"

Lena taunted her. "Yep."

I instantly intervened before my home became the next episode of WWF Smackdown. "Amber, just leave it alone. Lena, like I said. I'm not trying to take Jonelle away; I just want equal access to her. Yes, you've been a good mother to her, but I've also been there too. Don't make me out to be a monster."

"You are a monster! I wish I had never met you! But that's okay; I'll see y'all in court. And I bet when all of this is through, not only will I have sole custody of my daughter, but you will be paying more money in child support *and* this sham of a marriage will be over! I got something for you, Eric, and you're not going to like it!" Lena whipped her head around quickly causing her auburn, flat ironed hair to fly through the air like one of those Pantene commercials. She stormed out of the house, making sure to slam our front door in the process.

I looked over at Amber who was seething. I knew if I had not been there, a catfight would have surely gone down. Amber cut her eyes at me and said, "I don't care what you say, I'm calling a lawyer. That woman is not going to keep disrespecting me, especially in my own home." Amber mumbled something under her breath and walked towards the kitchen. She was going to the fridge to eat, indicating she was really furious. Amber was a classic emotional eater which meant that tonight and maybe tomorrow, I was in the doghouse, again.

The next day, I tried to forget about the Lena drama and focus on expanding Hayes & Ross Realty. The first order of business was meeting with Jay to discuss another property we had viewed a couple days before. The space was in Midtown off of Centennial Parkway, which was a great location, but the asking price was almost three times the amount of the Little Five Points property and the building wasn't as big.

Jay sat across from me, reviewing a listing of commercial properties near the downtown area that I had created exclusively for her. After flipping over the final page, she said, "This whole process is so exhausting. I wish someone could do this all for me, but one of the reasons my gyms are so successful is because I am the one that picks the locations. I have a knack for selecting the perfect place. If I left this up to one of my employees, they would totally screw it up; I know it!"

I nodded my head, understanding her dilemma. It was the same as mine. At that moment, I would have preferred to be at home, getting back in good with my wife, but I didn't trust leaving Jay in the hands of anyone else. I had to make this deal work; my success depended on it. "This process can be very trying, but when it's over, you'll be glad you hung in there. So, how are you feeling about the two properties we've seen so far?"

She smiled, revealing recently whitened teeth. "You know that I simply adore the building in Little Five Points. It's just hard for me to pick the first thing I see. I have to at least look at a few more before I'm certain that this is the right choice."

"So you didn't like the one off Centennial?"

"It was okay, but I wouldn't be getting as much bang for my buck, you know?"

The term "bang for my buck" was one that Amber used often when making a big purchasing decision. I contemplated picking up a dozen roses for her on my way home. I looked up at Jay who seemed to notice that I was zoning out. "I completely agree. The Five Points building is more economical," I said, trying to save myself.

It didn't work. She frowned. "You seem a little distant today. Is everything alright?"

"Yes, everything is fine. Just got a few personal things I need to work out, but it's nothing for you to worry about."

She stood up from the mahogany, leather, wingback chair and walked up to my desk. "You know what you need?"

"What?"

She playfully poked me in my arm with her right index finger. "You need to get out and have some fun. When's the last time you've been somewhere fun?"

I leaned back, trying to remember the last time I really relaxed. "Uh, my honeymoon in February. We went to Jamaica."

"Jamaica's cool, but that was what . . . eight or nine months ago? You know what they say. All work and no play, makes Eric a dull boy."

"We'll get out soon, but right now my wife's pregnant so we are taking it easy."

"Easy-cheesy! Boring! You know what? I've got it. How would you like to attend Magic Johnson's All White Party with me?" Her face lit up like a Christmas tree.

Magic Johnson was having a party in the "A?" I would have loved to go, but it was out of the question. "What? No. I can't."

She danced around my desk in excitement. "Yes, you can. You must go. It's by invitation only. It's the biggest party in Atlanta! Everybody who is everybody will be there. Celebrities, politicians, businessmen; you can't afford not to go. Do you know what this could do for your career? I'll even introduce you to some major players in the ATL. I'm telling you, if you go to this party, Hayes & Ross Realty will become the highest profiting commercial real estate company in Georgia within a year!"

My eyes widened. Wow! It was exactly the big break that I needed. Her words sounded so good I could literally taste them. "Seriously? This party is that big?"

She plopped back down in the chair. "Yes, so you're coming, right?"

I wanted to, but I knew I shouldn't. "When is it?"

"In two weeks. I can only bring one person, so I'll add your name to the guest list. Promise me you're coming and you won't back out. I'll never forgive you if you flake on me."

"I don't . . . I mean, I'm not . . . Oh, why not? OK. I'm in," I said, giving in. This party was a great business opportunity, and I would be a fool to let it pass me by.

"Fabulous!" She jumped up out of her seat and dashed toward the door. "It's at 7 PM, the Friday after next. Just meet me here at your office, and I'll have a car take us to the party. These types of events, no one actually drives to them. Dress code is all white, of course. Oh, and one last thing . . ." She raised her hand and wiggled her ring finger. "I don't want to look like I'm some home wrecker who's out with a married man. Please lose the ring, just for the party. Thanks, sweetie!"

My jaw dropped in shock and words eluded me. By the time I reconnected with the alphabet, she was gone. I banged my head against the desk in misery. She expected me to take off my wedding ring. Amber would surely kill me! How could I have ended up in this crazy situation? I considered calling her right then and telling her I couldn't go with her, but then I might have lost her business. I was shoulder-deep in personal problems; I didn't need things falling apart at work, too.

"I told you that woman was trouble." I heard a male voice interrupt my wallowing. I twisted my neck to see Carl standing at the doorway grinning.

"Not now, Carl."

"Okay. But when you're ready to do the smart thing and pass her onto someone else, let me know. You know how to reach me. Got my cell on me 24/7." He chuckled and strolled down the hallway toward the break room. Maybe he was right, but there was no turning back now.

Lesson 8: Hang In There!

Love endures long and is patient and kind; love never is envious nor boils over with jealousy, is not boastful or vainglorious, does not display itself haughtily. (I Corinthians 13:4)

"Last week, we discussed the importance of having love," Martin said the following Monday. By the time I got to the class, I felt a bit overwhelmed by the brewing chaos in my life. I had an upcoming court date with Lena in five weeks. Jay expected me to go to Magic's party without my wedding ring, and Amber was having a miserable pregnancy, which meant she loved me one minute and hated me the next. I felt like the only females in my life who weren't giving me a hard time were my daughter (who I rarely saw) and my mother (whom I called or who called me on a regular basis).

"Many of us are probably guilty of trying to accomplish things in this world without having love, without God. No matter our good intentions, the Bible tells us that without God's love in us, everything we do is worthless." Martin strolled across the room, one hand rubbing his chin and the other, holding his Bible.

"OK, we know we need to have love, God's love working in us. So what is love? How do we know when we are operating in love? People tell us all the time that they love us and then they turn around and hurt us. They lie to us, cheat on us, talk down to us. That can't be love, right? So what is this thing called love that we must have to make what we do count? And what is this thing called love that God is calling us as men to do for our wives?"

Martin picked up his Bible and waved it in the air to indicate that the Bible was the answer to the questions he was posing. "Let's look at what the scripture says in I Corinthians 13:4. Take out your Bibles and follow along . . . 'Love endures long and is patient and kind; love is never envious nor boils over with jealousy, is not boastful or vainglorious, does not display itself haughtily.' I know I just messed some of you up already. Go ahead, take a moment, and read it again to yourselves."

Familiar with this passage in the Bible, I reread the verse to myself and then looked up awaiting his interpretation.

Martin cocked his head to the side. "Love endures long. So," he paused, "which one of you is tired of your wife and thinking about getting a divorce? Based on the Bible, that's not love because love endures long. But wait, we can't stop there. It says that love endures long *and* is patient *and* is kind. Y'all still with me?"

We all nodded or grunted to let him know that we understood.

"This scripture is deep, so let's break down each part of it," he stated excitedly. "We have love enduring long, being patient, and being kind. Endure means to last, to tolerate, to bear, to hang in there. With this word endure, there is a timeframe connected to it: long. What is the duration of my toleration, lasting, putting up with what I have to deal with? The answer is for a long time. Love endures long, but not only does it hang in there for a long time, but while it is hanging in there, it is both patient and kind. See, this is what is messing some of us in this room up right now. We are enduring and we might even be enduring long, but our endurance does not include patience and kindness.

"Before I get ahead of myself, let's define patient and kind. Patient or patience is another term to describe endurance or tolerance, but it also implies a sense of waiting and being calm. If I am patient with someone, I am not only hanging in there or tolerating that person, I am also doing so in a calm manner that demonstrates that I am willing to wait on the person and let him or her do things in their own timing. A patient person does not rush or force someone or something, but allows natural progression and flow to decide when change will come."

A couple of "Amens" were spoken by men in the room.

"Finally, there's this word kind. Kind or kindness means to be caring, gentle, compassionate, sympathetic, and thoughtful. When people are kind to you, they are nice to you. Nice or kind behavior is positive. If I am kind, I am not being harsh or rude. I am not yelling or cursing you out. My words and behaviors are gentle and show that I care for you.

"So we merge these three attributes: endures long, patient, and kind. In other words, love is tolerant and will hang in there for a long time, waiting calmly for change, and behaving with care and gentleness. Now, let's make it practical. We have Brother Chuck here who is married to Sister Sara. Sister Sara always forgets to get the oil changed on her car, and every time Brother Chuck gets in her car, the check oil light is on, and oil is extremely low. Brother Chuck just bought this car a year or so ago and is paying $500 a month on the car note, so he definitely doesn't want to ruin the motor because of a lack of oil. Some of y'all right now are looking at me like you are already to wring Sister Sara's, a.k.a. your wife's, neck about this oil!"

We all laughed, many of us probably could relate to the scenario; I knew that I could.

"But love says no, we are not going to wring Sister Sara's neck because she's going to kill the car. We're not going to curse her out or tell her how stupid she is. We're not even going to make her walk to work or catch the bus until she learns how to check the oil. We are going to endure long and be patient and be kind. We are going to treat her with care and show her repeatedly how to check the oil. We are going to remind her exactly what that oil indicator means. We are going to check her oil every month to make sure she isn't running low. We are going to say kindly, 'Baby, I know you don't know a lot about cars, but if you drive around with no oil, it's going to mess up the engine which will mean you won't have a car to drive anymore. You don't want that to happen, do you? Well, if that light comes on, you tell me so we can add oil or get your oil changed.' And if she forgets again, we are going to once again tolerate, wait calmly for her to understand, and be gentle."

I heard a few sighs from brothers who seemed to not like the idea of being patient and kind. It was a struggle for me as well, but I was willing to work on it.

"I can tell by looking at you all that I just ruined your night. Some of you are thinking that there isn't that much endurance, patience, and kindness in the world. But there is. God demonstrates it every day toward you."

He was right. God was patient and kind to me, to all of us. It was only right that we demonstrated that behavior to others, especially our wives.

"Okay, moving on so we can get through this verse tonight. The second part of the verse says that love is never envious nor does it boil over with jealousy. If right now I told you all that your wives or girlfriends were at dinner with their ex-boyfriends, this room would be empty. There would be twelve vehicles riding down Interstate-20 like you all were Batman, driving the Bat-mobile, on the way to save Gotham City from The Joker. Jealousy."

Another outbreak of laughter was heard from the group.

"Some of you can't handle that your wife has a better job than you and makes more money. Jealousy. It might be somebody in here that doesn't even like for anyone to say anything nice about their wife because they are so tired of everyone singing her praises. Jealousy. Boiling over with jealousy. That's not love, brothers. Love says I trust you, and I'm not tripping about your ex-boyfriend. I'm your husband. I am the one you said I do to. For those of you in here who are not married, if she's not your wife, like the song says, 'If you liked it then you should have put a ring on it.' Why are you walking around here, trying to control what your girlfriend does when you haven't even fully committed to her? You're still playing games, but you want her to pretend she's your wife when it's convenient for you. Jealousy."

Martin shook his head slowly. "Love is not jealous. You should be happy when your wife is doing well, making money, and getting praise. That means that you also are doing well, making money, and getting praises. Marriage is two becoming one, so whatever good happens for her, happens for you too."

He glanced down at his Bible. "The last part of the verse says that love is not boastful, vainglorious, or does not display itself haughtily. All these words have to do with being conceited, prideful, stuck-up, thinking you're all that and a bag of chips. Love does not show off. It does not walk around saying, 'Look at me, look at me!' There are men, maybe someone in this room, that parade their wives like she's a trophy. These men only marry a woman so she can make him look good. These men think they are better than others, and they are only concerned with keeping up appearances. These men are the type of people quick to brag about all that they have. Brothers, this is not love."

I left class that day thinking about Martin's words. Love was patient, kind, and endured long. Love wasn't jealous. Love wasn't conceited or proud. I had heard this verse a zillion times, but I had never truly thought about what it meant for me or to me. I had never stopped to think about how God loved me and how He expected me to love others. But from the night's lesson, I had learned that God wanted me to treat my wife with kindness and patience that endured, even through her mood swings, stubbornness, and overbearing ways. She was trying to become better, and so should I. Dealing with Lena was a challenge as well, but I knew that God would still want me to behave in a loving manner, despite whatever she threw at me concerning Jonelle. It was going to take a lot of work and prayer, but I wanted to be in line with God's will, so I would give making amends my best effort.

When I returned home, Amber had seafood from Red Lobster waiting for me in the kitchen. She was wearing a black, satin nightgown that hung close to her slightly protruding belly. I kissed her passionately on the lips, not minding getting her sticky lip gloss smeared all over my mouth and chin.

"Hey to you, too," she replied once I backed away.

I washed my hands, grabbed a plate, and uncovered the Styrofoam to-go containers. "Awe, baby! You even got the cheddar baby biscuits! Girl, that's why I love you," I said happily before I began to fill my plate with bread, shrimp, crab legs, calamari, and mashed potatoes.

She giggled. "First of all, there's no sense in going to Red Lobster if you aren't going to leave with the biscuits. And secondly, so this is what I have to do to get you to love me? Buy some food?"

"I love you for the lingerie, too," I teased.

She picked up a glass of water from in front of her and said, "Keep talking junk, and I'll dump water over your biscuits since you love them so much!"

I covered my food with my hands. "Stop playing! Okay! Okay. Put the water down."

She rested the glass back down on the table and smiled innocently.

I grabbed her hand closest to me and kissed it. "Baby, thanks for dinner and for signing me up for the Husband 101 class. I wasn't sure about it at first, but it's turning out to be pretty cool and it's giving me some things to think about. Amber, I want you to know that I truly love you."

She didn't reply verbally, she just grinned and squeezed my hand. That's all she had to do. I knew she loved me too.

Lesson 9: What Goes Up Must Come Down

Rejoice not when your enemy falls, and let not your heart be glad when he stumbles or is overthrown. (Proverbs 24:17)

When I pulled into my driveway on Wednesday, a familiar looking silver Jaguar was parked in front of the garage, preventing me from being able to park my car inside. Annoyed that I had to park outside, I entered the house, looking for Tisha or another one of Amber's friends to ask them to move their car so that I could get into the garage. I rushed into the living room, but was frozen in my tracks by the last person I ever wanted to see sitting in my living room as if he were a part of the furniture, none other than Jonathan Gold.

I know it's not Christ-like to hate people, but I truly hated this guy. There was something about his overly confident aura that made my blood boil. The moment he saw me walk in, he gave me a cocky grin as if to say, "Yeah, I'm in your house, talking to your wife. What are you going to do about it?"

I shot him a DMX, y'all-gonna-make-me-lose-my-mind-up-in-here scowl, which he caught and must have completely understood. His grin fell slightly, letting me know that he wasn't crazy or sure of my mental stability. Amber must have witnessed our nonverbal faceoff because she was the first person to speak up. "Hi honey," she greeted me. "You remember Jonathan Gold, don't you?"

"Yes, I remember him," I replied dryly. "I remember him very well. What's going on, Amber?"

Amber begged me with her eyes to be polite. "Gold is interested in sponsoring some of the families that my daycare serves, more specifically the single parent households. Since I'm not supposed to go to work, I asked him to come here and talk to me about his offer."

When I didn't respond, Gold took the opportunity to explain further. "Mr. Hayes, my company is very eager to help others in the community, and we really applaud what Amber is doing through Sunrise Sunset Daycare."

I maintained my look of disapproval. "I see. Well, your Jag is parked in front of my garage so as soon as you get the chance . . . you know . . ."

"Actually, I think we're done here for now," Gold said, taking the hint. "Amber, thanks for accommodating me and please let us know what you decide." He stood up and grabbed his jacket. "Mr. Hayes," he said in recognition to me as he nodded and walked past me and out the front door.

"Eric, you know that was really rude." Amber lifted herself from the sofa and came closer to me.

Unbelievable, I thought to myself. "What's rude is having your ex-fiancé in our house when I'm not here."

"What are you trying to say, Eric? You think I'm cheating or something? I'm pregnant. Who wants to be with a pregnant woman?"

"A lot of men, trust me!" As smart as my wife was, at times she could be really naïve. Some men didn't care about a woman being married or pregnant. And men like Gold always wanted what they could not have.

She sucked her teeth and mumbled, "Whatever."

Amber moved from the living room into the kitchen and started taking food out to prepare for dinner. I followed her, still unconvinced about Gold's visit. "What did he have to say to you that was *so important* that he had to come to our house?"

Amber began cutting a head of lettuce. "You remember the Green Global business deal that they wanted me to do last year that I backed out of? Well, I was right; it went totally south. Gold's company got caught up in a lot of unethical practices. Their reputation is completely trashed."

I was glad to hear that life wasn't so perfect for Mr. Perfect himself. "So what does that have to do with you?"

She began scooping the cut lettuce into a big, plastic bowl. "They are trying to do a lot of community service to save their company's public image. They figure if they can show customers and the media that they really care about others, they can once again retain a positive reputation, which will lead to an increase in business."

"I feel bad for the guy, but it's his fault that he and his partner wouldn't listen to you, and I still don't trust him. I'm not comfortable with you having anything to do with him or his company." Honestly, I didn't feel that sorry for him. He had gotten what he deserved. Regardless of his situation, I didn't want Amber hanging around him.

Amber brushed her hands together to wipe off bits of lettuce that were stuck to them and then spun around to face me. "Are you trying to tell me that I can't let him sponsor the families that I work with?"

I shrugged nonchalantly. "I'm just telling you how I feel."

She let out a heavy sigh. "I know that he made some bad choices, and because of them he has to deal with the consequences. But we have all messed up at one point or the other. There are many stupid things that I've done over the years that could have ruined my career. Truth be told, there were many bad decisions that I made that negatively affected my personal life. You can't walk around with that kind of attitude, Eric. It's very judgmental. What happened to him could happen to anyone, including you. You need to stop acting so self-righteous because you're not perfect either, and one of these days, one of your little flaws could catch up with you, too."

I couldn't believe what she was saying to me. Was she actually rationalizing his dirt? And to make matters worse, did she really just turn it around and put it on me, like I was the bad guy? "Oh, so now you're sticking up for him instead of me, your husband? I didn't say that I was perfect; I'm just saying that it's his problem, and I don't want you involved."

She opened a bag of shredded cheese and dumped what was left of its contents into the bowl. "You know what, Eric? I'm not having this conversation with you. I'm going to make dinner and eat. You can join me if you want or not, but you're not going to tell me how to run my business. You have your own business. Do I tell you what to do at the realty? No. I trust you, and you need to give me the same respect." She dismissed me and continued to make a fresh salad as if I weren't in the room. After ninety seconds of being ignored, I grudgingly left the house, jumped into my car, and headed toward I-20 East. If she didn't want to talk to me, I would go somewhere where my presence was always valued. I headed to my parents' house.

I sat at my mother's kitchen table eating homemade chicken and dumplings while I told her how I had walked into the house and found

Gold there, alone with my wife. Because I was in mid vent, and it felt good to let it all out, I continued on in my rant to include my frustrations with Lena and how I rarely got to spend time with my child. My mother sat quietly at the table, watching me eat and listening to me spill my guts, shaking her head in shame from time to time at my circumstances. By the time I finished talking, my bowl was empty, and Nessy had taken off her wig.

"You don't really think anything is going on between Amber and Gold, do you?" she asked while she ran her hands over her real braided hair that could breathe now that the wig had been removed.

I wiped my mouth with a white paper towel. "No, Amber's not like that. If she wanted him, she would have married him instead of me. It just bothers me that he won't go away, and she's acting as if it should be okay for him to stick around. What if I were thinking about doing business with Lena? How would she feel about that?"

"Like I always say, these young girls don't know how to keep a man. Your father never had to worry about another man being in his house because it never happened. Even when the repair guy came to the house, he would let him in, not me. Mm. So what do you plan on doing, Son? Are you going to try to keep her from working with that guy?"

"I don't know, Mom. I don't like it, but Amber is not someone that can easily be controlled." I sighed. "I just feel like I got fifty pounds of weight on my shoulders. This whole baby process is really making our marriage difficult. Amber was always a moody person, but now it's like living with Dr. Jekyll and Mr. Hyde. I mean, it is non-stop emotions all of the time. One minute she is fun, and we're laughing then the next she's angry enough to spit nails. I thought she was going to kill

Lena when she showed up last week acting like she was just released from the loony bin. Amber was—"

"Are you out here whining again? Seriously man, go home and lay down the law at your house!" Nelson stepped into the kitchen and looked at me with pure disgust. "You need to man up. Matter-of-fact, come on, let's go." He gestured me to get up and follow him.

I peered at him suspiciously. My brother Nelson was another person who could not be trusted. "Go where?"

"We're going to your house to tell Amber that you're the boss and she needs to get in line."

The image of us approaching Amber, saying something disrespectful, and both getting slapped upside the head flashed through my mind. "What?"

Nelson began laughing. "Man, I'm just playing with you. You should've seen your face! That woman got you on a tight leash; doggone shame. Nah, let's go for real. Come with me to the pool hall. It's time you hang with some real men because your pink panties are showing."

Thirty minutes later, Nelson and I were finishing our first round of pool at Moe's Pool Palace and talking with two of his old high school friends, Rocky and Wes. Wes was on his second marriage, but even that one wasn't working out too well. Rocky thought he was a player, like Nelson, but he had about six or seven kids by four or five different women. They were cool to hang with, but as far as I was concerned, none of them were in a position to give me relationship advice.

"Y'all gotta help my baby brother. He's messing up the game for all of us!" Nelson complained to his friends. "Out there trying to be all committed and serious about a woman, letting her run the house.

Next thing you know, all of these women are going to expect this kind of behavior from the rest of us."

Rocky and Wes laughed, but I didn't see anything funny. It was a mentality like Nelson's that kept women believing that all men were dogs, when this concept wasn't the truth. There were a lot of good men like me who just wanted to take care of their families and get ahead in life. Obviously, the crew that stood before me wasn't included in the "good men group" I was referring to.

"Yo dude," Rocky started. "I respect you being married and everything, but these women will take your manhood if you let them. For real, I know what I'm talking about. I got five baby mommas, and they all try to control me. That's why I'm not married. If I could find a woman who would just chill out and let me handle my business, I would marry her, settle down, and do the whole little house with a dog thing. You know?"

What in the world was he talking about? I didn't have time for any loser philosophy. "No, I don't know. You know you sound dumb, right?

"Whoa! I sound dumb?" He pointed his pool stick at me. "I'm just trying to school you, help you out."

I laid the stick that I was using against the wall. "No disrespect, but how could any of y'all help me? Rocky, you're always running from child support, Wes, you get married every decade, and Nelson, you're too scared to commit to a cell phone contract much less a woman. Is this really how you all want to spend the rest of your lives? If so, you can count me out because I've got a good life. I have my own business, a good woman, a nice house and car, a beautiful daughter, and another baby on the way."

Nelson sat on the edge of the pool table and chuckled. "You also have a crazy ex-girlfriend that never lets you see your child, a domineering wife that gave you her business so that you could feel like a man, and a nice car that your wife purchased for you! Get out of here with all of that 'I've got a good life' mumbo jumbo. At the end of the day, you've got just as many problems as the rest of us. The only difference is that we're man enough to tell these women to back off, and you're not."

These dudes were fools, and talking to fools only made me foolish. I was ready to leave. "Whatever, Nelson. I'm out." I grabbed my jacket from a nearby chair that it was lying on, slipped it on, and began to walk out. Before I could get past the table, Nelson reached out his arm and stopped me.

"Eric, you're my bro, and that's why I'm telling you the truth. These women will eat you alive if you let them. I know you got your wife and business and feel like you've moved on up like the Jeffersons. You think you're all that right now, but mark my words, it's all going to come crashing down on you. That's science, bro! What goes up must come down."

Lesson 10: Stop Acting Like A Clown

It is not conceited (arrogant and inflated with pride); it is not rude (unmannerly) and does not act unbecomingly. Love (God's love in us) does not insist on its own rights or seeking its own way, for it is not self-seeking; it is not touchy or fretful or resentful; it takes no account of the evil done to it [it pays no attention to a suffered wrong].

(I Corinthians 13:5)

By the following Monday, things had naturally smoothed out between Amber and me. We hadn't discussed whether or not she would allow Gold to donate to the families at Sunrise Sunset, but I decided not to press the issue. I didn't want to stress her out any more than I already had. She was already struggling with the idea of staying away from her business, telling me that she felt as if she was under house arrest. I figured since she was taking one for the team with this pregnancy, the least I could do was avoid aggravating her over my own trust issues related to Gold.

Once again, I sat in the rear of the class while Martin spiritually fed us more insight about love.

"I Corinthians 13:5 states, 'It is not conceited, arrogant, and inflated with pride; it is not rude, unmannerly, and does not act unbecomingly. Love, God's love in us, does not insist on its own rights or seeking its own way, for it is not self-seeking; it is not touchy or fretful or resentful; it takes not account of the evil done to it, it pays no attention to a suffered wrong.' Brothers, verse five is loaded with information. Notice, this is the second week in a row that we are only studying one verse instead of multiple verses. As we move through the class, you will find this will happen often. Why? Because this thirteenth chapter of Corinthians has few verses, yet each of them is powerful and filled to the brim with wisdom and insight. It reminds me a lot of men and the way we frequently communicate. Most of us are not talkers; we really don't have a whole lot to say. Our wives or girlfriends may bug us about communicating more, but we prefer to keep many of our thoughts initially to ourselves. Nevertheless, when we finally are ready to speak on an issue, those words we utter are powerful, and we mean them. We might only say a few sentences, but our thoughts and feelings about a matter are wrapped up in those few words."

Many of the fellas in the room nodded their heads in agreement.

"This appears to be the case with this chapter in Corinthians," Martin continued. "Very few verses, but they explode with truth. We are forced to slow down and really pay attention to what the writer is saying about this thing called love.

"Last week, we discussed a bit about love not being conceited, so we won't spend too much time on the first part of the verse, but I want you to at least make a mental note of the fact that once again the idea of love not being conceited is brought up again. Obviously, the Apostle Paul wants us to truly understand that arrogance has nothing to do with love. Arrogance is something often connected to men, especially men that have a certain level of success or achievement. It is very easy for us to get caught up in what we have or think we have and become prideful and puffed up about it. But love is contrary to this type of behavior and mentality. If you think you're 'the man' and are operating out of that energy, you are not reflecting God's love in you."

The image of Gold sitting in my living room flashed through my mind again. He was the epitome of arrogance, and the thought of him made my chest burn. I really needed to let my negative feelings about him go, but something inside of me couldn't seem to get beyond the intense dislike.

"The second aspect of the verse says that love is not rude and doesn't act unbecomingly. Unbecomingly is a nice and proper way to say acting like a fool, or as I call it, a clown. If you are running around the house screaming at everyone, if you are cutting your wife down in front of folks or making sly comments to her family and friends, if you are racing up to her job causing a scene in the parking lot, and if you are calling people in her cell phone contact list trying to find out who she is talking to, you are out of order and not from a place of love. It's a bunch of clown-like behavior. The next time you find yourself getting ready to lose it and act like you should be locked up somewhere, tell yourself this: Love does not act unbecomingly. Love has manners. Loves says good morning, goodbye, thank you, please, and may I. Love pulls out chairs, opens doors, and all that other chivalrous stuff that we've forgotten in the 21st century. Love says, 'No, you first.' And I'm going to hit you hard with this next one, brothers; love says, 'I love you, too.' I know you all might not like that mushy stuff, but when your woman tells you that she loves you, and you know that you love her as well, say it. Stop being rude and acting like she she's speaking Italian. You heard her, so respond. Tell her how you feel. Don't leave her hanging. You want her to tell you good things, and she deserves the same. Stop acting like a clown."

Maybe Martin was right. Maybe I was acting like a fool when it came to Gold and Amber. She had picked me to be her husband, so there was no reason for me to feel so insecure when he came around. Furthermore, she trusted me, so I should have been giving her the same courtesy. But then again, she didn't know about Jay or my promise to attend the upcoming party with her. I had no doubt that if she knew; she would be the one acting like a clown, instead of me. I had been mulling over and over in my head how to back out of the engagement, but it was useless. I either attended the party with Jay and ring-less, not only to keep her business, but also gain future opportunities, or I cancelled on Jay, and all of my hard work over the past several months went straight down the drain. I was stuck between a rock and a hard place, and time was running out. The party was on Friday, a white tuxedo was in the closet at the office, and Jay had already texted me earlier today confirming the time she would pick me up. Feeling defeated, I attempted to blink back the worry and pay attention to what Martin was teaching.

"The verse goes on to say that love is not self-seeking. It does not insist on its own way. Okay, some of y'all may not come back to class after tonight. I can see that right now."

Several men in the class, including myself, laughed.

Martin also laughed. "But seriously, how many of us have to have our way? Men, we can be harsh like that. It's either our way or the highway. If she doesn't want to do things the way we want or like, she has to go, or we're leaving. We feel we can find another woman who will give us what we want. That's not love, y'all. Love is not self-seeking, which means if I love you, I am not going to force my way upon you. If I love you, I can respect that you may have a difference of opinion or a different way of doing things. As much as I may think my way of thinking and operating is superior, I am willing to let you choose on your own without me dominating everything. And if I love you, I am not going to demand things from you. I am not even going to demand that you love me back. The choice is yours. God doesn't demand our love. No. He gives His love freely to us whether we decide to take it or not. We get to choose. Love is not based on receiving love back. When you love someone, you love them regardless of whether or not your love is ever returned. Stop being mad at someone in your life because you loved them, and they didn't love you back. Love is not self-seeking; it does not only love people who love back. Love loves because it does, end of story."

Yes, I'll admit, I wanted my way when it came to Amber, so Martin's words hit me like bricks. I immediately felt guilty, knowing that I wasn't acting out of love by trying to force her to handle the Gold situation my way. Thank God, I hadn't listened to those knuckleheads Nelson, Rocky, and Wes, or I would really be in a bind right now. They would have had me packing my bags and living back with my parents, trying to find a woman who would bow down to my every command. That wasn't what I wanted. If so, I would have never married Amber. I was aware from the moment I said 'I do' that Amber would always speak her own mind and march to the beat of her own drum, and I loved her for it.

Martin looked down at what appeared to be his written notes and said, "Love is not touchy, fretful, or resentful. In laymen's terms, love is not sensitive, easily or constantly offended, or highly irritable. Some of you all, everything your wife says gets on your nerves. Some men just stay mad, just stay annoyed. Come on! We can't have good relationships with the people we care most about if we always have an attitude about something. We have to learn to let go of the grumpiness, the discontentment, the resentment, and everything else that's keeping us from being close to our woman; we've got to let it go.

"Finally, the verse ends saying that love does not keep tabs of wrongs done against it. Now, I know that women are really good at keeping track records. They will bring something back that we did twenty years ago and throw it in our faces. But brothers, we do the same thing. The only difference is that they say it, we don't. We remember the pain that they caused us, we just don't verbally say, 'You did this and that.' Instead, we will hold it against them. We will always remember it. We won't truly forgive and forget about it. In our mind and memories, we are counting."

The room grew quiet enough to hear a pin drop. Martin waited a few seconds before continuing, "God separates our sins, our wrongs from us, and says He remembers them no more. It's like it never happened. He wants us to do the same. Whatever your wife, your girlfriend, or anyone else that you love did to you, count it as forgotten. Burn the records. It's over. That's how you strengthen your love in a relationship; you forgive and forget. As long as you're holding on, you can never experience love the way God intended."

Forgiveness. Such a simple word that was so hard to do. I wasn't the type to hold a lot of grudges, but I did have a few, namely Lena and Gold. I knew God was watching me so it was time to start the road to leaving the past behind me. I had to practice forgiveness if I wanted to be forgiven by God. I hoped that people in this world who needed to forgive me could do the same. I also hoped that I would be forgiven for my future sins, like the one that I would commit that Friday.

Lesson 11: Success Has A Price

The earnings of the righteous (the upright, in right standing with God)
lead to life, but the profit of the wicked leads to further sin
(Proverbs 10:16)

On Friday evening, I stood in front of the mirror in my office's private
bathroom, trying to muster up the courage to take off my wedding
ring. *Just for the party. Just for one night*, I told myself. *This is just
business. Anyone in your position would do the same. You're not
cheating. You're not doing anything wrong.* Then why did I feel like
the moment I took off this ring, I was going straight to Hell?

I am not claiming that I've never sinned or more specifically never
cheated; I had done both in my life, but I had never cheated or even
considered doing anything remotely close to cheating since I'd been
with Amber. Though going to a party with another woman who was a
client from work wasn't technically cheating, it still was deceitful. If it
was honest, I would have been able to tell my wife about it. Instead,
she was at home with her friend Tisha, watching movies and believing
I was attending a business dinner party with a *male* client. I never told
her that my client was a male; I simply said it was a client named Jay,
knowing she assumed Jay was a guy. I lowered my head in shame. I
was definitely going to Hell with gasoline underwear on after tonight.

I spun the ring around my finger several times. I was dressed to
the nines, white tux and all, looking like I just stepped off the set of an

old school, Boyz II Men video. I had visited the barbershop earlier that day, making sure my hair was low and my shave was clean. I smelled like a mixture of Ivory soap and Polo cologne. The only thing left to do was remove the wedding band from my ring finger, but my conscious wouldn't let me do it.

My cell phone rang. It was Jay, saying she was outside. It was time. My mind went blank, and I did the first thing that came to it: I pulled the ring off of my ring finger and slid it onto my middle finger. It was a silly alternative, but I just couldn't completely go without it. Jay would have to accept the last minute compromise.

I exited the building, greeted the driver who was holding the back door to the white Maybach open for me, and eased into the expensive car. I sat next to Jay who, of course, looked stunning in a white strapless gown accessorized with Swarovski crystals. After offering her a quick hello, I looked out the window, ignoring the urge to check out the vehicle's refined interior. As much as I was a car junkie, at that moment I felt like the biggest, dressed up, low-life in the world.

Jay must have sensed my discomfort because she said, "Eric, just relax. This is going to be one of the best nights of your life."

I glanced at her, gave her a half smile and a double nod, and then returned my eyes back to the moving view of the window.

She giggled, causing me to turn back towards her. "So I guess your middle finger is the best you can do, hunh?" We both looked down at my left hand, my platinum band securely placed on my middle finger while an imprint remained where it used to be, on the finger next to it. "It's OK. I get it. You're a nice guy who wants to be faithful to his wife. That's rare these days. I really appreciate you coming with me and trying to accommodate me. So why don't we shake off all the apprehensions and go make you Atlanta's next millionaire?"

I looked up into her eyes. She appeared sincere as if she was truly interested in helping me to grow my business. I blocked out my worries and decided to make the most of the evening. I was in a car, a Maybach at that, on my way to an exclusive party with the most distinguished people in the south. It was time for me to stop feeling sorry for myself, put on my game face, and make power moves.

"Thanks for inviting me," I responded. "You're right. Let's do this!"

The party was incredible. Everybody, I mean everybody who was somebody in Georgia, was there. Jay had been right; actors, actresses, singers, politicians, athletes, billionaires, and even royalty and dignitaries from other countries were in attendance. True to her word, Jay shuffled me around the huge ballroom, introducing me to various wealthy people as the best realtor in the ATL. I gave out a bunch of business cards and received just as many. Several people asked me to contact them the following week about personal and commercial properties they were interested in buying or selling. I even got to meet Magic himself! Took a picture with the man and everything!

By the time, we pulled back up to my office at 1 AM, I was dazed and spent. I had never worked so hard in my life. It was a party and a lot of fun, but rubbing elbows with high society was ridiculously draining. The car pulled up to the curb, and the driver got out and came around to my side. He waited before opening the door to allow me to exit.

"So did you have fun?" Jay asked, still looking as refreshed as she did when she picked me up earlier that evening.

I smiled brightly. "Yes, yes, yes! Oh wow! It was fantastic. Thank you *so* much for talking me into going. I've been praying for something this big to happen to me, I just never thought it would actually happen. I owe it all to you. Thanks, Jay."

She leaned closer and placed one of her hands on my knee while using the other to trace a soft line down the side of my jaw. My facial muscles tightened underneath her touch. As much as I was attracted to her, physical affection was not the ending I was looking for.

"I could make all of your dreams come true," she said seductively in a raspy voice. "I know you're married, and I don't want to cause any problems, but just think about it. For me." She moved even closer and kissed me gently on the cheek, right where her hand had been. Then just as smoothly as she approached me, she eased away and retuned back to her side of the backseat.

"Good night," I replied anxiously. "Thanks again." I knocked on the window, signaling the driver to let me out. He complied, opened the door, and then shut it behind me after I was firmly on the sidewalk. As the car pulled away, I wiped the side of my face where she had kissed me. If I weren't married and deeply in love with my wife, I would have taken her offer, right then and there. But I wanted my marriage, my unborn baby, and everything else Amber and I had built together. *Maybe going to the party with Jay wasn't such a good idea after all.* I took a deep breath, sucking in the cool night air, and headed to my car.

I hoped Amber would be sleep by the time I returned home, but she wasn't. She was lying in bed, reading a book. She watched me as I entered the bedroom and began to remove the formal clothing.

"You look very handsome," she said. "I didn't know it was a fancy affair. I could have come with you." She closed the book and rested it on the night stand next to her.

I pulled off my shoes and socks. "Thanks. It was something I sort of had to do on my own."

She nestled deeper into the comforter, only leaving her face uncovered. "I understand. So how did it go?"

I took off my tuxedo jacket, tie, vest, and dress shirt. "It went very well. I actually met quite a few important people who want me to contact them about real estate. I just hope that they remember who I am next week when I call."

"They will. I'm really proud of you, baby. It's great to see that you've really taken the business to a new level. I'm glad I trusted you with it." She smiled at me tenderly.

"Yeah, me too." I removed my pants and t-shirt, leaving on only my boxers. I turned to head into the bathroom to take a quick shower before climbing into bed.

"Babe?" she called out.

I stopped and looked back at her. "Yeah?"

She lifted herself up from lying down to sitting up. Her face instantly changed into a frown. "Why is your wedding ring on the wrong finger?"

I looked down at the platinum band, still positioned on my middle finger. "Oh, that."

Busted.

Lesson 12: Love Is The Truth

It does not rejoice at injustice and unrighteousness, but rejoices when right and truth prevail. (I Corinthians 13:6)

"For a month now, we've been talking about this thing called love," Martin stated at the beginning of our next class. "We've discussed how God is calling men to love their wives as Christ loved the church. From there, we began to study I Corinthians 13, examining the traits and definition of love. I know this is a lot of information to digest, and if you are really taking this class seriously, it should be affecting your relationships with others. So this week, I'm going to go light on you all. We are going to go over one short verse, and then I'm going to dismiss you all so that you can catch the Monday night football game. I know many of you might be sacrificing your ESPN time for this class, so we are going to reward you for staying committed thus far."

I know you're probably wondering how I got out of the whole ring drama with Amber. I can tell you this, it wasn't easy. I don't have a whole lot of experience with lying, and I can't say that I'm the best at it because I'm not, but when backed into a corner, my lies sometimes come out fairly believable.

"Why is your wedding ring on the wrong finger?" she asked.

I looked down at the platinum band, still positioned on my middle finger. "Oh, that." I slid the ring from my middle finger and put it back on my ring finger. "Now, it's in the right place." I laughed, really out of nervousness, but I tried to make it seem as if it were a you're-never-gonna-believe-this laugh. "I had a few drinks tonight for the sake of business, and you know I'm not a drinker. One of the guys asked me about my ring and I took it off and showed it to him. He's getting married soon or something like that. Anyway, I must have put it back on wrong and just didn't notice because of the alcohol in my system." The words came out my mouth so quickly that I didn't even realize I was lying until I had already said them.

"Oh," she responded, still seeming a little unconvinced. Having no evidence to refute my excuse, she was forced to accept it. "You probably should stay away from drinking from now on. You don't have to drink to conduct business. Just be yourself."

"Yeah, you're right." It was all I could say. I felt so ashamed. This whole situation with Jay had me lying to my wife, and that wasn't who I was. I lowered my head and exited the room into the bathroom, seeking the escape of a hot shower. As I let the heated water fall over my head, I prayed and asked God to forgive me and to help me get back on the right track.

I looked forward to Monday night's class because I desperately needed to feel closer to God. My actions lately had been deceitful and questionable, and I felt as if I was slowly losing control over my ability to make good decisions.

"Let's turn in our Bibles to I Corinthians 13:6," Martin said, regaining my attention. "It reads, 'It does not rejoice at injustice and unrighteousness, but rejoices when rights and truth prevail.' Read that verse again to yourselves."

I read the verse again in my Bible awaiting his explanation.

"This verse may seem simple, but it really is not. Among all of these lengthy and information compacted verses, we have this short, fifteen word verse. Shouldn't there be more to it? The statement is simple, but its meaning is profound. Love celebrates the truth.

"Some people will lie to you and tell you it was for your own good. Some will withhold information, hide things from you, steal, cheat, and say that they did it to protect you. There are people in this world that say they love God, but they will abuse, misuse, and destroy others. But love does not rejoice at injustice or unrighteousness. Love does not condone evil. Love does not affiliate itself with wrong doing or anything that is a lie. Love only cheers for truth and for what is right.

"There are a lot of us who rationalize our wrong doing, using the excuse of love. 'I love my wife, so that's why I lie to her about my drinking, my gambling, or that other woman.' Or how about, 'What my wife doesn't know won't hurt her.' And we cannot leave out this one, 'I think I'm in love with this other woman, and if loving her is wrong, I don't want to be right.' Let's be real, family. This is not love; it's selfishness, and it's sin. Love rejoices with the truth. If there is something you are deceiving yourself or your woman about, it's time to come clean."

Martin closed his Bible and said, "I will let you all go home, but someone in here may need to forgo the football game and deal with freeing yourself from the lies. It's time to tell the truth and to live in truth because love means being about the truth. Let's keep it 100 percent real from now on."

If it weren't for the class filing out of the room in front of me and me looking silly for sitting there alone, I would have never gone home.

Martin had said the very words that I needed to hear. There was no question in my mind that that lesson had been for me. I was a liar, and I justified my lies, thinking that the truth would hurt my wife, but in reality, it was the opposite; my lies would hurt her more. I had been completely selfish. I was more concerned about my hurt and my loss rather than Amber's pain. Loving my wife meant being honest with her, even if the truth didn't feel good.

I spent the rest of the evening staring aimlessly at the TV screen, the game seemingly unexciting. My thoughts continually drifted back to coming clean with Amber and telling her the real reason behind my late night and misplaced ring. By the time the game went off, Amber was fast asleep, but I knew what I had to do the next day. The Bible says in James 5:16 that we should confess our sins to one another so that we may be healed and restored. From the outside, my marriage looked solid, but I knew that on the inside, it was slowly crumbling, and we hadn't even made it through the first year. Denial was the place where marriages really died; when people saw the symptoms of decay but just pretended as if they were not there. If I wanted to save my marriage from eventual destruction, I would have to start making changes now before the cracks and holes became irreparable. The first step would be telling Amber the truth, even if it meant breaking her heart.

Lesson 13: Confession Is Good For The Soul

A [consistently] righteous man hates lying and deceit, but a wicked man is loathsome [his very breath spreads pollution] and he comes [surely] to shame. (Proverbs 13:5)

I spent the majority of my workday mentally plotting how I would confess to Amber about going to the party with Jay the woman, not Jay the man. I also intended to tell her how Jay had come on to me. I realized that I was taking a huge risk, that Amber might not only accuse me of lying and cheating, but also forbid me from working with Jay ever again. Regardless of Jay's immoral behavior towards me, I still wanted her business badly.

I recognized that walking away from the commercial deal with Jay was probably wisest for my marriage, but I had never been so close to accomplishing something so major. It seemed like every time I found myself approaching a life goal, some unexpected circumstance arose and kept me from crossing the finish line. That was the case with going to college when I was a bit younger. I was in the middle of my junior year when my father had a heart attack. Of course, he survived, but he was unable to go back to work for a while. The job he had didn't offer much paid sick leave, and it took a few months before his disability check kicked in. My mother was an emotional wreck. Although I am the youngest in my family, my older siblings either refused to or couldn't step up and help out my parents, so I quit school, took on two jobs, and stuck around the house to support my parents during their crisis. My mother didn't want me to stop attending school, but I wouldn't listen. They needed me, so I did what I had to do.

Now years later, I didn't regret my decision, but I still mourned my departure from college without a degree. I often ran into old college friends who did finish their Bachelor's degree and some who went on for graduate degrees as well. Every time they talked about their jobs or their education, sadness crept into my heart because I always thought I would be there with them, singing the same tune. I planned to return to school, but life happened, and there was constantly a need that kept me away from going back.

Thinking about my failures caused me to feel more strongly about making current opportunities, like the one with Jay, work. I desperately needed to accomplish something grand so that I could feel as if my life actually mattered. Maybe I wasn't paying enough attention during the Husband 101 course. I heard all that Martin was teaching about us loving our wives, yet I couldn't help but wonder where me loving me fit into the picture. Why couldn't I just love myself this time and do what I needed to do for me? Why did everyone else's wants and needs constantly seem to supersede my own? Why did it appear that being a man was about being responsible for the whole world? Every problem, every crisis, every mistake in society was blamed on men. I had been hearing my entire life, "A man should do this," and "A man is supposed to be that," but in reality, the pressure to be a great leader didn't feel empowering; it just felt heavy.

Jay called me midday, confirming our appointment to meet at 4:00 PM at another property from the list I had generated for her.

Feeling guiltier, I decided to call Amber at 3 o'clock, before I went to my meeting with Jay, to get the truth out in the open. I figured that if she flipped out, I could always meet with Jay and tell her that I could no longer work as her realtor. I took a few deep breaths as I waited for Amber to answer the phone, attempting to calm my nerves.

"Hey babe," she answered sounding cheerful. I hated to rain on her parade with my confession.

"Hey, sweetheart. Um, baby, there's something I need to talk to you about. You got a minute?"

"Yes and no. Tisha's on her way over and should be here at any second. We're going to go look at some baby furniture. Is everything OK?"

She didn't have the time to talk, but I needed to say it before I lost the little bit of courage I had built up. "For the most part. I, uh . . . Let me ask you something. I know you work with all kinds of people, including the opposite sex. How do you handle working with men, especially the ones that are attracted to you?"

She let out a half giggle, half grunt. "I don't know! What kind of question is that? I just set boundaries, I guess . . . Wait! Is this about me working with Gold? Are you really still trippin' about that? If it's that big of a deal, Eric, I won't work with him! But I think you're being very selfish about this."

OK, this wasn't going at all the way I had planned. She was quickly assuming the wrong thing, but then again, I was a little glad to hear that she wouldn't work with Gold if I insisted. "No, Amber, that's not what I'm saying. It's not, I mean, yeah I really don't like the idea of you working with Gold, but that wasn't the—"

She cut me off. "Oh! That must be Tisha. She's driving so I don't want to keep her waiting. Sorry, for cutting the conversation short like this. Was there something else you wanted to say?"

"Well, I–"

"I'm going to kill her!" Amber interrupted me again. "She's outside beeping the horn like she's possessed. Okay, let me go, Eric before one of our neighbors gets upset."

I really wanted to tell her to make Tisha wait until I had the chance to say what was on my mind, but it was pointless. Amber was preoccupied, and I was no longer feeling brave. "Oh . . . OK. I'll just see you later on."

"Love you, babe. Bye!"

"Love you too." I heard the line click, and she was gone.

I remained quiet during our viewing of the commercial property on Martin Luther King Jr. Blvd., allowing the seller's agent to talk-up the space. Jay was in straight diva-mode (as usual) wearing body-flattering clothing, big designer shades, and killer high heels, while acting as if money was the name of her pet dog. Watching Jay interact with the other agent helped me to put our situation into perspective. Jay and Amber had a lot in common. They were both attractive women who knew exactly what they wanted in life. They both knew how to connect with people, both could run a business with their hands tied behind their backs, and both had a way of looking at a man that made him feel as if he was the last guy left in the world. It made sense why I would struggle with saying no to Jay and find myself "trapped" in her game. I was attracted to women like Amber and Jay; they were my "type." It was something about a woman who understood her worth that got my blood pumping. I still wasn't interested in having a relationship with Jay or cheating on Amber, but I could certainly understand why I was sure that Amber would never approve of me spending time around Jay if I ever mustered up the guts to tell her the truth.

As Jay and I were parting ways after the viewing, she turned to me and said, "Okay, I've seen enough. I believe I'm ready to make a deal on the Little Five Points property. Do you think you can make the offer for me?"

"Uh . . . yeah. Sure," I said, a bit taken back by her unexpected decision. Here I was contemplating how to cut her off as a client, and suddenly she was waving a big, fat commission check in front of my face.

"Good. I will call you tomorrow," she said, smiling brightly.

"Great." I shot back a fake grin and moved toward my vehicle before she could say anything else. The stakes had changed, and now there was no way that I could tell Amber about my temptress client. I simply needed to hold on to Jay's business for maybe another thirty days so we could seal the deal. Then I could go back to being the honest husband I was known to be. I just needed one more month.

Lesson 14: Love Can Handle It

Love bears up under anything and everything that comes, is ever ready to believe the best of every person, its hopes are fadeless under all circumstances, and it endures everything [without weakening].

(I Corinthians 13:7)

I spent the rest of the week following up with my new contacts from the All White Party and working on Jay's sale. It was late October and Thanksgiving was coming up in a few weeks, which meant many people were slowing down on business transactions in preparation for the holidays. Thankfully, I was able to schedule several appointments for early January with new clients from the party. Mr. Parke had accepted Jay's offer, the paperwork had been completed, and we were now just waiting on final approvals and processing from the banks. If all went as planned with Jay's acquisition and my new connects, my dream of turning Hayes & Ross Realty into a well-known commercial realtor would come to fruition.

By Monday, my life felt as if it was starting to look up. Not that I had a bad life, but for a while chaos seemed to be taking over. I still had my upcoming court date with Lena, and I still would have to make it through closing without any more incidents with Jay, nevertheless, according to my calculations, by Christmas, both of these issues would be settled, and Amber and I could move on with our lives minus the drama. I actually looked forward to attending class that evening.

Martin's lessons constantly challenged my thinking, and although I wasn't making all of the necessary changes in my behavior yet, I found myself having a strong desire to become a better man.

"I Corinthians 13:7 reads, 'Love bears up under anything and everything that comes, is ever ready to believe the best of every person, its hopes are fadeless under all circumstances, and it endures everything, without weakening.' I'm going to admit, brothers, verse seven is my favorite verse in this chapter. Why? Because after the writer discusses the specifics about what love is or is not, he then comes to verse seven and tell us all that love can do." Martin paced across the front of the room, his Bible in one hand, and using his free hand to gesture as he spoke.

"Let's go back and compare. Before this verse, the previous verses were reading, 'Love is this' or 'Love is not this.' Now we move away from that kind of language and are thrown into a description of just what love is capable of. The King James Version of the Bible simply says, 'Beareth all things, believeth all things, hopeth all things, endureth all things.' It's like the description of love isn't complete without letting us know the limitations of love, or actually lack thereof." Martin was excited, and his enthusiasm over the scripture seemed to energize all of us.

"How powerful is this statement? 'Love bears up under anything and everything that comes.' The word under signifies that love is actually the one holding up the full weight of the matter. If you can, imagine in your mind a bridge. Bridges are created to hold up cars and people so that they can get across from one side of land to another. Due to their purpose, bridges have to be made strong enough to withstand heavy weight and harsh weather conditions. If a bridge cannot last during a storm or rush hour traffic, it's not a very good bridge, and it's useless. With that image in mind, know this: Love is stronger than the strongest bridge. God's love working in us is able to withstand any and everything that comes along. There is nothing too hard or too heavy for God's love. When we talk about love isn't enough, we are deceiving ourselves and others. Love is enough. The problem is that we are not operating out of love; we're operating out of ourselves. Listen closely when I say this, brothers: There is nothing, nothing that love cannot handle, but we've got to let love bear it, not ourselves. We can't take it; we're weak. But love, love is strong enough. Nothing, including death, is too much for love to handle."

Martin peered down at his Bible. "The verse goes on to say that love is ever ready to believe the best in every person. I think this is one of the biggest problems that holds us back in today's society. We don't believe in anyone or anything anymore. We think everyone is bad and out to get us. We don't think others or even ourselves can change. This is why when a spouse commits a sin against us, we struggle to forgive them. We are so afraid that they are unable to change and, therefore, we hold the offense against them because we think that they will do it again. We don't believe anymore, and the enemy uses our disbelief to keep us from ever enjoying life and others the way God intended.

"But I'm here today to tell you that it's time to believe again. I'm not saying that people won't hurt you because many will. But love says that even if you hurt me, I still believe the best in you. I still know that you're a child of God and that He created you to be better than this, and if you only reconnect with His love, you will return to being your best again. Believe in your wives; believe in your girlfriends and fiancés. Stop thinking so negatively. Maybe the reason they keep disappointing you and hurting you is because you believe that's what's going to happen anyway. Faith has the power to move mountains, but if our faith or belief is negative, it also has the ability to move things in the opposite direction. You make matters worse when you speak your unbelief. We know that life and death are in the power of the tongue, but then we say things like, 'Oh, I know she's cheating. Oh, she ain't gonna ever marry me. Oh, she isn't a good wife; I don't know why I married her.' You speak these things because you believe these things, and this is exactly what you are getting. Believe the best in your women because that's love. Start believing today, and I guarantee you'll start seeing the difference in your marriage."

Several "Amens" were uttered from class members. I nodded in agreement.

"Then verse seven states that love's hopes are fadeless under all circumstances. Hope has to do with our expectations and confidences. So the verse is basically saying that when I am operating in God's love in me, I have the capacity to hope or expect or be confident in good things no matter what is going on around me. Have you ever met someone who is going through the bleakest situation, but still believes in a good outcome? I mean everything is falling apart, but the person still has hope and still expects to come out on the other side OK. Look at Job from the Bible. He lost everything, all his money, possessions, children, even his health. But he never lost his hope. Job had God's love in him, and we can have that same love that produces that same level of hope in us.

"Finally, the verse ends stating that love endures everything without weakening. This is often an issue for couples. We get together, and everything is wonderful. Then we go through hard times in the relationship, and difficulties begin to chip away at the bond we once had. One day, we wake up and say to our girlfriend or spouse that we've been through too much and the love is now gone or not strong enough anymore. When we do this, we are not reflecting God's love. God's love in us has the ability to endure everything and continue to love just as strongly as it did at the beginning. It doesn't fade or weaken or chip away. Yes, brothers, you can still love your wives as much as you did on your wedding day even twenty years later, after all hell has broken loose in your home when you are operating out of God's love in you. God's love, regardless of the circumstance, remains strong."

As always, I left class that evening feeling a mixture of convicted and revitalized. God wanted me to step up in my love, appreciation, and commitment toward Amber, and I wanted to comply, but I often found myself putting my career goals ahead of my marriage. I struggled with knowing what the proper balance should be between a husband providing financially for his family and being there emotionally for his family. I kept trying to persuade myself that my recent distancing from Amber was only temporary and necessary so that we could have more as a unit. Each time I left the class, I was confronted by my conscious, telling me that if I kept moving in the direction that I was moving, one day I would look up and not know who or where I was.

Lesson 15: You're No Better Than The Rest

Many a man proclaims his own loving-kindness and goodness, but a faithful man who can find? (Proverbs 20:6)

I hadn't heard from my mother in several days, which was unusual. Nessy and I had a very close relationship, speaking to each other by phone at least every other day. I sensed something was wrong. I tried to call her, but the answering machine kept picking up. My parents weren't scheduled to go out-of-town, and if they had left for any reason, they would have called me to let me know where they were.

My stomach turned as I left the third message in three days. I had been so busy with work and taking the Husband 101 class that I hadn't been back to my parents' house since a few weeks prior, when I was upset with Amber about Gold. On top of everything, I had attended a couple of meetings with the lawyer Amber hired for the custody case, some woman named Ms. Sherri Greene. Supposedly, Sherri, Amber, and Tisha all went to college together. Sherri was now a successful attorney who specialized in family law and had won 90 percent of her cases. I just prayed my case wouldn't be one of the unlucky 10 percent.

Feeling uneasy about my parents, I left work early and headed to the Atlanta suburb of Conyers to find out why Nessy and Dwayne weren't returning my calls. During the ride, I called my sister Karyn, to see if she had heard from my parents.

"What's up, big head!" Karyn answered.

"Nothing, duck face! Have you heard from mom or dad lately?"

"Uh, yeah. I saw her yesterday."

I frowned. "That's strange. She hasn't called me or returned any of my messages. Is she okay? I'm on my way out there now."

"Well . . . she's just going through right now. That's all I can say."

"Going through what?"

"That's for her to tell you. If you're going out there now, you'll find out when you get there. Don't panic. It's not a matter of life or death, well, not really."

My heart started to beat faster. "Okay, Karyn, you're scaring me. Something's up with Mom, and you're acting all secretive! Seriously?"

"She asked me not to tell anyone, including you. So that's for her to tell you. That's all I can say."

"Thanks for nothing, Karyn. I'll talk to you later." I hung up the phone, annoyed and anxious. My conversation with Karyn confirmed my fear that something was wrong with my mother. I didn't understand why she wouldn't call me and tell me, and why she would choose to confide in Karyn instead. I felt as if I couldn't get to my mother's house fast enough. I was already doing the speed limit, but I pushed down harder on the gas pedal, praying no police officer would catch me doing twenty miles over the limit the rest of the way to Conyers, Georgia.

Twenty minutes later, I pulled into the driveway of my parents' three-story, red brick home. My father's car was not there, but my mom's was, so it was likely that she was there. Using my key, I let myself into the house, calling out her name so that she would know that it was me. She didn't respond so I proceeded to look in each room for her, starting with the main level, moving to the second level, and ending in the basement. When I didn't find her on any of the levels, I considered leaving before a final thought crept into my mind: the patio.

I opened the patio door to find my mother sitting in a cushion-covered patio chair, staring aimlessly out into her mostly withered garden. It was the beginning of November, and although the weather in Georgia was mild in comparison to the rest of the country, nothing colorful was growing in Nessy's flower garden. I expected her to acknowledge me and invite me to sit with her, but as I closed the door behind me, she still hadn't even twisted her neck in my direction. It had to be really bad. The word "cancer" screamed in my head; however, I refused to say it or even believe it until she confirmed my worst fears.

I sat down in an empty chair across from her, not knowing how to start a conversation with her. That was a first. I could always talk to my mom, and when I couldn't, she always took the lead and talked to me. I could share everything with her, my dreams, my failures, my thoughts; very few topics were off limits. Now we sat in silence, a wall of unspoken problems creating a valley between us. She had a secret, and I had mine. She didn't know about Jay, and I didn't know about . . . *What didn't I know about her?*

"Ma," I said to her. She blinked so I knew she heard me. "Ma, what's wrong?"

Nessy's eyes watered, and I thought she might cry, but right before enough water built up to cause the tears to run over, she closed her eyes and blinked the salty solution back down. Instead of responding with words, she took a deep breath in and slowly released it.

"Ma," I said again once it was obvious that she wasn't going to answer. "You're scaring me. Please talk to me. Please tell me what's wrong. I'm not leaving until you do."

She nodded and sighed. After another minute of silence, she found her voice. "Your father is a good man, but he's not a perfect man. He's gotten better over time. There's so much you kids never knew about him, so much you never saw because by the time you got old enough to understand, God had changed him."

I jumped up out of the seat. "Did something happen to Dad?"

"Our first few years of marriage were really hard on us. We were young and didn't know what we were doing. We started having children, and it was a lot on both of us. One day, your daddy came home and he wouldn't look at me. I knew something was up, but he never said anything. For a while, maybe a few months he was different, and then one day, he was back to the man I loved; everything was back to normal. I always thought that he might have been unfaithful, but I was too afraid to make him tell me the truth. So I let it go and acted as if I didn't doubt him."

Confused, I sat back down in the chair. *Dad cheat on Mom?* I couldn't imagine that idea tied to my father's name. But my mother appeared so crushed so obviously she believed it to be true. "Come on, Mom. Do you really think dad would cheat?"

She looked out into the distance. "A letter came in the mail last week. I was right all along. Your father had been unfaithful back then. Some . . . married woman he knew whose husband was in the military. And the worst part . . . the woman had gotten pregnant by your father, but never told him or anyone. She led her husband to believe the child was his. They moved to California and raised this child, a girl. All these years he had another child out there and no one knew. She is older than you."

"How do you know this? Is she here? Are you sure?" I asked, my voice somewhat raised higher.

She sighed again. "I'm sure. The girl, well she's a woman now, wrote the letter. Seems that her mother's husband always knew the truth. He passed away recently, and before he died, he told her what her mother never would; he wasn't her real father. She went to her mother and forced her to tell her about your dad. She says she just wants to know us and that she doesn't want to cause any harm. That's funny. She already has caused harm. I have to find a way to forgive my husband for something that happened decades ago, and it's not easy."

I cupped my face in my hands. An outside child? Secrets? Infidelity? It was all surreal. "Where's Dad?"

"He's staying at your Uncle Robert's house for a few days. I just needed some time alone."

I reached over and placed one of my hands over one of hers and squeezed. "Are you going to be OK?"

"Eventually, yes." She finally looked at me; sadness filled her eyes. "I won't pretend that this isn't hard for me. All this time I thought that if I was a good wife and mother. Nothing like this would ever happen to me, but like the Bible says, time and chance happen to us all. It just hurts."

"Are you . . . going to leave him?"

"No."

"No?"

"Eric, I'm not going to lie to you; I have thought about leaving, but what good is that going to do? I love your father, and punishing him now for something he did over forty years ago, well, I would just be punishing myself. Whether a marriage survives is not about the mistakes made, and there will be mistakes, but our ability to make up after the mistakes."

I walked into the house that evening, devastated. I had looked up to my father for so long. It hurt me that he had been unfaithful to my mother, but I couldn't judge him because I hadn't always been the most honorable man myself. However, the fact that he was careless and got another woman pregnant was what I struggled with getting over. I couldn't believe that I had another sister out there, that another woman who wasn't one of my known two sisters could claim that our dad was her dad. I wondered if Nelson knew anything about this turn of events. If so, he was probably somewhere patting him on the back and welcoming him into the players' club. The thought of it all made my head hurt.

Amber was sprawled out on the couch, watching a Lifetime movie and eating Lays potato chips. The moment she saw me walk in, she threw a final chip in her mouth and sat up. "Aaaaa," she moaned. "I'm going to die in this house! Do you know I've watched seven straight hours of Lifetime and have eaten two whole bags of chips? Who does that? Who eats two big, family size bags of chips in one day? Lays wasn't lying when they said you can't eat just one. It's ridiculous. I feel fat and bloated and bored. I want to go back to work!"

I shook my head at her. Under normal circumstances, I would have laughed at her, but tonight, laughing wasn't an option. Instead, I plunked down next to her and grabbed the three-fourths eaten bag of chips from her.

"OK. Something is wrong. What happened?" she asked, observantly.

"Honey, I really don't want to talk about it." I reached into the bag, pulled out a few chips and munched on them.

"I respect that, but you probably need to talk about it. So just tell me the short version."

I dug into the bag again. "The short version? Fine. My father cheated on my mother before I was born, and he and my mom just found out that he has a love child from this affair. That's the short version." I devoured several more chips.

"Oh." Amber scooted closer to me and wrapped one of her arms around my shoulders. "That's a lot to take in. Eric, I'm sorry you're going through this. Is there anything I can do to help you or make you feel better?"

I looked at her and gave her a half-smile. "No, but thanks."

"How's your mom taking it?"

"She's pretty hurt."

She rubbed my back gently. "What about your dad?"

"I haven't seen him. He's staying over my uncle's house for a few days while things calm down. I just can't . . . I just never thought something like this would happen to my family. This is the kind of stuff you see on TV. On Lifetime! How did we become a Lifetime movie?"

I could tell that she wanted to laugh at my statement, but she restrained herself and kept a straight face. "You know, they base those movies on real life stories. The craziest tales are based on someone's real life. Are you going to talk to your dad?"

I moaned. "Honestly, I really don't want to. I feel so let down. This is going to be a hard one for all of us to forgive."

"But you have to forgive him, Eric. You remember last year when I was going through it with my family and you helped me to give them another chance. From experience, I know that dealing with parents and forgiving them for what they did or didn't do is not easy, but if you don't let it go, you'll be stuck just like I was for all of those years. And you'll miss out on being close to them and being loved by them. He made a bad decision, but life goes on, and we've got to keep moving forward even in times of trouble."

She was right; I didn't want to be bitter because of a refusal to forgive. I had seen what holding on to pain could do to people; it made them miserable. I wanted to go back to the way things were before this news, but I wasn't sure how to face my father again. My mother was willing to try to stay with him; I wondered if Amber would do the same. If I had slept with Jay, could she still love me? I had been raised to believe adultery was a cardinal sin, one of the acceptable reasons to get a divorce, but was there such a thing as love and trust despite an affair? Was this what Martin meant by love enduring and bearing all? I turned towards her and gazed into her eyes. "Would you forgive me? If I ever cheated or did anything like this, would you forgive me? Would you stay?"

"Eric, this isn't about us—"

"She's going to stay with him. I just want to know if you would."

She rested her head on my shoulder. "I don't know. I wish I could say yes, but that's one of those things that you don't know until it happens to you. I pray it never happens to us."

I wrapped my arms around her and held her close. Tonight, my parents had shown me that even good marriages have to go through the fire. I prayed my parents really could survive the scorching flames, and even more, I hoped my marriage could, too.

Lesson 16: Love Stays

Love never fails [never fades out or becomes obsolete or comes to an end]. As for prophesy (the gift of interpreting the divine will and purpose), it will be fulfilled and pass away; as for tongues, they will be destroyed and cease; as for knowledge, it will pass away [it will lose its value and be superseded by truth]. (I Corinthians 13:8)

By Monday, I was still moping. I intended to visit my father and talk to him about the affair, but I hadn't got over the initial shock yet and was afraid that I would blow up at him if I saw him. Truthfully, I was so upset that I didn't want to attend the Husband 101 class, but Amber thought it would be good for me to get in a positive environment and get my mind focused back on God's Word. Sitting in the class, I was glad I had come. In typical "Almighty God fashion," the message seemed directed at me and for me.

"I Corinthians 13:8 reads, 'Love never fails, never fades out or becomes obsolete or comes to an end. As for prophesy, the gift of interpreting the divine will and purpose, it will be fulfilled and pass away; as for tongues, they will be destroyed and cease; as for knowledge, it will pass away, it will lose its value and be superseded by truth.'"

Martin held his Bible tightly in one hand and looked up at us, all twelve of us still committed to coming weekly to the class. With his free hand, he rubbed his chin before speaking again. "Finishing off the discussion of the capabilities of love, the Apostle Paul writes that love never fails. It is followed in the Amplified Bible by a further explanation that love never fades out, becomes obsolete, or comes to an end. Everything in this world will eventually fail. Our government fails, our physical structures fail, relationships fail, and even nature fails, but love, God's love, never fails. There is no end to it, it never fades, and it never becomes outdated or unnecessary. With God's love working and living in us, we are also able to express that kind of love towards others, including our women. We are able to love them in a manner that is endless and timeless. People are often awed when they hear of marriages that have lasted fifty or more years. Why? Because we see love as a temporary state, as something that fades away over time. It is difficult for us to imagine spending half of a century with the same person, but God's love in us can last to the end of time and beyond. It makes me think about that old Heatwave song 'Always and Forever.' The song contains lyrics such as, 'I'll always love you, forever, always, forever love you, and forever and a day.' Don't get sanctified on me now. I know you all know that song."

A couple of men in the front started singing a few lines of the first verse of the song before breaking out into laughter. The rest of us laughed with them then joined in, singing the song as well. By the time the group had sung the end of the last chorus, many of us were belting out the song with our eyes closed. After the group had calmed down again, Martin regained his professional stance and continued the lesson.

"The point is this: You can have love that lasts always and forever, but understand that that kind of love only comes from above. God resides in us, giving us the ability to love forever and a day, but we have to operate in His love and not out of ourselves."

The song and the message made me think about my parents. For them to continue on beyond this crisis, both of them would have to pull from God's love. My mom would have to be able to forgive and let go, and my dad would have to show his wife that he was repentant of his errors and still desired to spend the remainder of his life with only her. Now, understanding my father's part in bringing their marriage together again increased my need to visit him. I had to look him in the eyes to know if he really loved her, if he loved her enough to do the work that it would take.

"Verse eight then takes us all the way back to the first and second verses of I Corinthians 13 and reminds us of the limitations of everything else in this world." Martin walked slowly up and down the middle aisle. "Now, remember during the second class when we discussed everything being nothing without love. We talked about having the ability to speak and influence people with our words. We also talked about having the prophetic powers and having all of the knowledge in the world. Well, we are called back to these first two verses in the second part of verse eight. It tells us that prophecy will be fulfilled and pass away, tongues will be destroyed and cease, and knowledge will pass away. These attributes are being once again compared to love. At the beginning of the chapter, the comparison was that having these traits without having love made them worthless. Now, the comparison is that having these traits means having something temporary because none of them last forever. Love is the only attribute that will last, that is not temporary, and that will not pass away.

"Once again, we are reminded not to put our energy into aspects of life that do not include love, for these things without love are useless and will eventually end."

On my way out of the class, for the first time, I stopped to socialize with Minister Martin. Usually, I flew past him with a quick, "Good night," but today I felt the urge to thank him for the much needed encouragement. I had come to the class feeling defeated, but I was leaving with hope. The lesson had taught me that there was a way for my parents' marriage, as well as my own, to survive. That way was through God's love.

"Thank you for an inspiring class," I said to Martin as I paused to shake his hand.

"I'm just the vessel," he responded as he returned the handshake. "Thank God."

"Amen. I have really enjoyed the classes. They are giving me so much to think about and at a time when I need it most." A wayward thought crossed my mind. *You should talk to him about the issues you're struggling with. It helped Amber to talk to his wife, talking to him may help you, too.* However, I felt uncomfortable with the idea and attempted to disregard the thought.

"That's great news to hear. I know your wife was a little concerned that you might not want to participate, but I'm glad that hasn't been the case. By the way, how's Amber doing?"

"She's good. Going crazy because the doctor has her on bed rest. You know Amber, she does not like to slow down, but she's hanging in there, and I'm glad she muscled me into taking the class," I laughed.

Martin grinned and nodded. "Muscled? You certainly are married to Amber Ross. Lydia and I talk about you two all of the time. You know, Amber was her special student, the one God has kept heavy on her heart. Amber has grown so much since taking the Wife 101 class. I pray the same will happen for you too."

A small part of me wanted to confide in Martin about my parents' marital issues as well as my own, but I really didn't know him that well, and I was afraid he would respond to me with some old religious talk like, "There isn't anything too hard for God," so I hesitated. "It is helping me to change my perspective on marriage. I recently found out some . . . some things about my family and I . . ." I shook my head in defeat, knowing I wasn't ready to open up to him about my problems.

"Listen, you don't have to explain to me," Martin consoled, "but if you ever need a listening ear, I'm here. As men, we need other Christian men that we can open up to, people who are going to speak positively over our lives, men who will pray with us and hold us accountable. This is what the Husband 101 class is all about; strengthening each other so that we can be the kind of men God is calling us to be."

Relief washed over me. "I appreciate that, Martin, and one day, I will probably take you up on that offer."

"Anytime. Hey, my wife and I are renewing our vows on our anniversary, New Year's Eve. Lydia's probably already sent you all an invitation, but make sure you guys come. We would love to have you there."

"Okay. Amber hasn't mentioned it to me yet, but we'll definitely be there." I extended my hand for a parting handshake.

Martin clasped my hand within the two of his and shook it comfortingly. "Sounds good. Good night, Brother Eric. Remember, whatever you're going through, don't forget to pray about it. There is refuge in God's presence."

That wasn't the religious talk I had been expecting.

Lesson 17: The Pot Calling The Kettle Black

He who has no rule over his own spirit is like a city that is broken down and without walls. (Proverbs 25:28)

I needed to talk to my father. The situation hung over my head like a black cloud. Attempting to work was useless, and all of my staff noticed the obvious change in my behavior. It was like I was a zombie, walking around in their presence but not really there. Attending the Husband 101 class had helped–for that evening–but by the next morning, I was back to feeling . . . numb. I had held so much pride about my family being this terrific, ideal group of people who knew how to respect each other and stay together. Over the years, I'd watched my friends' families argue, break-up, and dismantle, but my family was strong. We were founded on Christian values, and we refused to be entangled in the enemy's plan to destroy the family unit. Until now . . .

I sat in my office, staring out the window at the half-covered trees, the periodic breeze, loosening more of the burnt orange-colored leaves, causing them to break away from the brown limbs. Positive and negative thoughts played in my mind. *God is in control. How could Dad mess up the family like this? Love is able to bear this. Maybe everything, including love, must eventually come to an end. Love never fades. What if I'm just like my father?*

"Eric!" The sound of my name pulled me out of my trance and back into reality. I spun around in my chair to face Carl, who was gaping at me like I was dying.

"Hey man," I replied.

"Dude! You are really trippin' lately. What's going on with you?"

"Nothing, I'm cool."

Carl shook his head. "Come on. You know I'm not falling for that. For real, what's up?"

"Just got some personal stuff going on, some family drama. Don't worry about it."

"Amber? Did she see you with Ms. Johnson?" He shot me a nervous glance.

I laughed. "No."

Carl sighed. "Eventually, she will. She's out in the lobby."

I sat up straight. "Who? Amber?"

"No, Ms. Johnson. She says she doesn't have an appointment, but she needs to speak with you."

I felt a headache coming on and unconsciously placed my hand on my forehead. "I'm not in the mood to deal with her today, but tell her to come on back to my office."

Carl pushed my office door closed to give us privacy. "You sure you don't want me to take over her file? Whatever is going on with you must be major because you never act as if you don't want to see a client, especially one this big."

I felt depleted. I looked up at Carl and shrugged. "I probably should have listened to you before and gave her to you, but what's done is done. She's decided on a property already so the hard part is over. We're just waiting on closing."

"Listen, even if it's just closing, I can handle it for you. If you've got something going on with your family, you need to prioritize home. This work stuff will always be here. I know I joke around with you often, but seriously, take care of home." Carl glared at me with eyes so intense that I could feel his concern penetrating from the sockets.

"I hear you." I didn't want to be alone with Jay; I was too emotional, and I might say or do something I would regret. Suddenly, seeing my father became urgent; I had to see him quickly before I completely lost my cool and sabotaged my business. "You know what? I need to go handle this personal matter so I will catch Ms. Johnson as I go out the door. Thanks, and if I need you to close on her property, I'll let you know."

I grabbed my jacket, closed up my office, and headed down the hall. Ms. Johnson, better known to me as Jay, was standing in the lobby with one hand on her hip and the other with a cell phone in it, pressed against her ear. The moment she noticed my approach, she spouted off a few directives to the person on the line and quickly disconnected the call.

"Jay, how are you? How can I help you?" I asked cordially as if the night of the all-white party never happened.

"I'm great. How are you?" she asked, ignoring my second question.

I was determined to avoid falling for her charm. "Actually, I'm a little busy. In fact, I'm on my way out the door. Is there something you needed?"

"I just wanted to follow-up with you on a couple of matters."

"Okay. How about I walk you to your car and answer any questions on the way."

She beamed. "Sure."

Hoping she wanted to discuss business, I instantly began to explain what was going on with the deal as we exited the building. "I still don't have an exact date on the closing yet. The bank has accepted your offer, but we're still waiting on paperwork on their side. I can call you when the date has been confirmed. I'm thinking it will happen in a few weeks or so."

"Lovely. What about my other offer?"

I stopped walking in front of her car. "What other offer?"

She giggled and flipped her hair. "Don't act coy with me, Eric. I know you're a very intelligent man. The offer I made you the night of the party."

It was exactly what I was afraid of. "Oh, *that offer*. Ms. Johnson, I'm—"

"Jay," she corrected me.

I nodded, consenting to her correction. "Sorry, Jay, I'm extremely flattered, but I'm married and I love my wife. I really don't want to do anything to hurt her and that includes having more than a professional relationship with you. You're a beautiful woman, and if I weren't married, I might consider it, but I can't. I hope you understand." I felt relieved that I had stood up to her and turned her down. I expected her not to like my statement, but to accept it and let the matter go. But she didn't.

"I do understand," she said, "and that's why I like you so much; you're so faithful. Eric, I'm not a woman who takes the word no easily. Actually, I never accept the word no. There is always a way to get a yes. That is why I am so successful; I believe in never settling for no. I will give you more time to think about it. And while you're thinking about it, think also about this: I'm attending a New Year's Eve ball at the White House. I'm at liberty to bring a guest. Let me know if you would like to be my date." Jay winked at me and jumped into her car before I could respond. She was halfway down the street before I realized that despite my rejection of her offer to have an adulterous affair with her, I still wasn't free of her antics.

Mulling over Jay's last words to me, I drove towards my Uncle Robert's house. She was being unfair. Of course, I wanted to go to an event at the White House, who wouldn't? But at the risk of my marriage? It was a low blow on her part, making me an offer that I couldn't refuse. Well, actually, I could refuse it, but it was difficult. She knew I was determined to build my company and my income. An evening at the White House could change my life; only God knew what business opportunities could result from it.

One thing Jay was right about, she could make ways for me that Amber couldn't. Amber had been the one to take me off the sidelines and give me a starting position, but Jay was someone who could take me from the playoffs and into the Super Bowl. If I were a different kind of man, starting an affair would have been a no-brainer, but I wasn't that type of guy, right? I thought my father wasn't that type of guy, but I'd been so wrong about that, too. Maybe we were all *that guy*; the one who loved his wife, but fooled around to get some other internal need met. That was why I needed to talk to my dad; I had to know his motivation.

My Uncle Robert lived in Lithonia, another suburb of Atlanta and about a fifteen minute drive away from my parents' home in Conyers. My father opened the door, let me in, and informed me that Uncle Robert and his wife, Olivia, weren't home. I entered the house and took a seat on the sectional sofa in the living room where my father was lounging and watching old reruns of *Good Times*. For the first few minutes, we both stared at the television as if I had come over to watch it with him. After several studio recorded laughs and a "Dyn-o-mite," I turned my attention to my father who simultaneously looked at me.

My dad was a man who usually bore a weary expression. He claimed it was a permanent reward from all of his years of slaving for "the man." Today, his tired face appeared even more beat, almost shattered. I realized then that he probably was hurting as well, but it was too much to ask for me to feel sympathy for him. He had put himself in this predicament, along with the rest of us.

"So you talked to your momma, hunh?" he began the conversation.

"Yeah." I wanted to say more, but my words betrayed me.

"And she told you about Denise?"

It was the first time an actual name was being used. I winced as I repeated it. "Denise?"

He looked down at the floor. "Denise, my other child."

A surge of pain ripped through my chest, giving way to my words. The truth was on the table, and he wasn't even contesting it. "I can't believe it's true. I can't believe that you really are admitting it!" I yelled.

He looked up at me with partially swollen eyes, tears in the midst of them. "Am I supposed to deny it? I know what I did was wrong, and these are the consequences that I have to live with."

I could tell that he was sorry, but I couldn't stop my hurt or my anger. "No! These are the consequences that we all have to live with, not just you! How could you do this to mom? How could you do this to our family?"

"Eric, Son, I know this is hard for you, but it was a mistake that I made a long time ago. I never wanted to hurt any of you, especially your mother." The tears gave way and a few of them rolled from the edge of his eyelids, down his rugged cheeks.

I saw his tears, but I resisted the desire to cry with him or even comfort him. If my mother was crying, I wanted him to cry too. So I took a verbal knife and cut him down again. "But you did, Dad. The worst part is that I always took pride in the fact that I was just like you. You were my hero, and I wanted to be just like you; have a family, take care of the bills, all of that. Now I am wondering how much like you did I become. Am I going to cheat on my wife too? Lately, I've been thinking about it. Got a perfect opportunity. I mean, she's a ten! Good looks, great body, smart, rich, everything a man could want. So should I be like you and have a little fling with her? What do you think, Dad?"

My father frowned at me for a second and then recomposed himself. "Son, I know you're upset, but you will still respect me." He released a heavy sigh. "I let you all down, and I let myself down. I've had to carry this burden all of these years, trying to be a good example of a man to you and your siblings when I knew I had messed up. I was hoping that it was over and that I would never have to face my failure again, but now, my dirt is back in my face, and it has a name: Denise. I can't hide from this thing anymore. I sincerely apologize to everyone.

"Eric, if watching me go through this will help you avoid making the same errors I did back then, well, thank God. You don't want this kind of shame, Son. Whoever this woman is that is acting as if she has it all is lying to you. If she had it all, she wouldn't be trying to get close to a married man. Good women, honest women, women with values, morals, and self-esteem don't want or need a married man. I let my head get all blown up, let my pride get in the way, and I wouldn't listen to what God was trying to tell me. Whoever this woman is, run from her."

I knew he was right, but my feelings wouldn't let me admit it or allow me to accept his apology. "No disrespect, Dad, but I won't be taking any advice from you from now on."

He looked away from me, and I immediately knew that I had said too much.

I calmed my anger a few notches and said, "I just . . . I just need to know why you did it, and please don't say something silly like you were young and dumb. Keep it real, Dad. Why?"

He continued to look across the room as if he weren't speaking to me, but I was the only one there. "I did it because I wasn't sure."

"Sure of what?"

"Sure of my life. I met your mom, and everything happened so fast. We got married and next thing you know we were having children, and it was like my whole life was being decided for me. I kept asking myself if this was the life that I really wanted, but I wasn't sure. I know that sounds selfish, but it was how I was feeling. And then I met Robin, and we both were confused about our marriages, and . . . I made a big mistake. Luckily, her husband got stationed out west, and I was relieved when she left because although we had already ended the affair, knowing she was around was killing me inside. She never told me she was pregnant. I swear I never knew."

"Did you ever become sure? About Mom? About us?"

"Yeah. After a little while, I knew where I really wanted to be. The affair . . . was exciting at first, but then it became empty. I saw how it was causing a rift between your mom and I, and I didn't want to lose my family, so I broke it off."

The room grew quiet with the exception of *Good Times* playing in the background. Ten minutes later, Uncle Robert and Aunt Olivia returned home, giving me an excuse to leave. I drove home uncertain of whether my father's confession had helped me or hurt me more. He cheated because he didn't know what he wanted, didn't know if he wanted the family my mother had given him. The truth stung, but being at odds with my father pricked my heart worse. I longed to demonstrate mercy towards him, to leave this whole situation in the past, but my pride wouldn't let me tell him that before I left. I was supposed to be upset with him, not making amends.

I thought about Jay and her attempts at tempting me. Although nothing had really occurred between us, I was in danger of compromising myself because I badly wanted the perks she could give me. It was then that I realized that most men don't cheat because we don't care about our significant other; we cheat because we are being self-centered and find ourselves consumed with something we believe we need. My father needed assurance, my brother needed emotional protection, and I needed achievement. But what about the needs of the people we hurt in the process?

Lesson 18: No More Excuses

But when the complete and perfect (total) comes, the incomplete and imperfect will vanish away (become antiquated, void, and superseded). (I Corinthians 13:10)

"This week, we're going to look at two verses, I Corinthians 13:9-10. Please take out your Bibles and follow along," Martin said at the start of class the following Monday.

I was starting to cope with the idea of having another sister and my dad's exposed affair. I hadn't spoken with either of my parents since I'd left my Uncle Roberts house the week prior, but a call from my sister Karyn had informed me that my dad was back at home with my mother. I felt mixed emotions about his return home. On one hand, I was glad that they were working out the problems in their marriage, but on the other, his exile seemed too brief. I wasn't surprised that my mom had let him back in so quickly; she hadn't slept alone in close to fifty years. She probably figured, why start now?

A part of my decision to reclaim my sanity was linked to my custody hearing scheduled one day away. Since the blow up several weeks ago, I had not seen or heard from Lena or Jonelle. I tried to call Lena a few times, but my calls were sent straight to voicemail. I knew Lena was infuriated about having to go to court, and her way of tormenting me was to end all communication with her and our daughter. My response was to fight fire with fire; I reported her behavior to my attorney and geared up for a nasty legal battle.

Martin cleared his throat as he smoothed out the page in his heavily used Bible. "It reads, 'For our knowledge is fragmentary, incomplete and imperfect, and our prophesy, our teaching, is fragmentary, incomplete, and imperfect. But when the complete and perfect, total, comes, the incomplete and imperfect will vanish away, become antiquated, void, and superseded.'

"We've been studying the characteristics of love, its importance, and its capabilities. We've been comparing love with other qualities that are desirable, yet inferior, to it. Now we come to a slight shift in the message. Reading these verses alone or out of context, it would seem as if the writer is finished with discussing love, and that he has moved on to another topic. But if you look down a few verses to verse ten, you will see that once again, the word love and its importance are discussed. So obviously, the writer has not completed his teaching on love, and we can come to the conclusion that, in fact, these verses, verses nine and ten, as well as the two following, still are related to understanding this thing called love."

I nodded my head in agreement and understanding as I followed along.

"Now knowing that these verses are about love, we can look at them again with new eyes and a fresh perspective." He peered down at the Bible and continued. "Verse nine refers to our imperfections. Notice it uses the word 'our' multiple times. The word 'our' differentiates between God and man. God's knowledge and prophesy or teaching is complete and perfect, but ours is not. If we link the idea of love into this statement, we come to glean that God's love is compete and perfect, yet ours is not. His ability to know love and share love is perfect, lacking nothing, but ours has holes, gaps, and spaces.

"When we continue on to verse ten, it tells us that there will come a time when perfection and completeness will come, and that which is imperfect will vanish away. We have already addressed that God is the only one who is perfect and complete. So when God comes, He is able to perfect us, to remove the imperfections in our lives, including the limitations in our ability to love. A first glance at these verses, it is easy to think that they are referring to the Second Coming of Christ or when we get to Heaven; and it does. However, I am inclined to believe that they also reflect our lives now. God isn't coming, He is here! The Word says, 'His love in us,' meaning that He is already here and offering us the chance to perfect our loving, even now. We are capable of expressing perfect love because He dwells within us."

A few "Amens" went up from the group.

"Brothers, what I want you to take with you from these verses is this: Don't use that tired old excuse, 'God's still working on me.' The work is already done. All you've got to do is empty yourself of you and let Him reign as Lord over your life, and He is able to demonstrate His perfect love through you towards your wife who is also His bride. Yes, on your own you are incomplete, imperfect, destined to fail, but with God in you and working through you, you are a man and a husband that is able to love your wife as Christ loved the church and gave His life for it. You can, even right now, love as God loves because He is in you, giving you the power and ability to be complete in your loving. You just have to believe it, receive it, and move out of His way. Surrender to His love, brothers. No more excuses."

I took Martin's message to heart. I believed that I could be complete in my loving not just in the future, but right away. I went home that evening desiring to show my wife a more loving husband. Amber looked at me as if I were mad when I pulled off her socks and began to rub and moisturize her feet. Many times she had requested that I do this simple task for her, but not particularly caring much for feet, I refused to comply. Now that massaging her toes had become an act of love, I found a smidgen of pleasure doing the task, especially as she smiled in delight and let out a few "ahhhs" for her pampered, swollen feet.

"What's come over you?" she asked as I replaced her sock on her left foot and prepared to repeat the process on her right one.

I grinned confidently. "My love for you."

She laughed. "My love for you? You know that's really cheesy, right?"

"Just like the smell of your feet, but hey, I'm rubbing them anyway."

We both laughed.

Amber looked at me caringly. "So are you ready for court tomorrow?"

"As ready as I'm going to get. I haven't heard from Lena, so there's no telling what she has up her sleeve, but I'm pretty sure that it's a bunch of lies to destroy my character."

"Maybe, but don't worry about her. Just tell the truth, and God will work out the rest." She wiggled her lotion topped toes. "*And* if a beat down is in order, I think I can handle that part!"

"I bet you could." I stopped caressing her foot for a moment. I felt the need to come clean with Amber about Jay, but I wasn't sure how or where to start so I eased into it. "I'm glad we're talking about the truth. There's been something on my mind for a little while now that I want you to know. I have a female client who has been coming on to me. There's nothing going on between us, but she has expressed her interest. Baby, I told her that I was married and wouldn't do that to my wife. You know I wouldn't do that to you, right, Amber?"

She tilted her head, angelically. "Babe, it's OK. Thank you for your honesty, but you don't have to tell me every time a woman makes goo-goo eyes at you. It's going to happen. You're an attractive and smart man, and other women are going to see what I see. If they didn't see it, I would be nervous that maybe I was making you up in my head!" She giggled. "Men hit on me all of the time, but you're my man so they don't even matter."

"Who hits on you? It better not be that Gold guy, that's all I know," I said, trying to sound hardcore.

We both laughed, again.

"Gold's not crazy. He knows how much I love you. And he knows that you'll knock him out."

"True."

She pulled her foot away from me and sat up a bit more. "Uh, I think we need to pray for our family because between you and me, we have way too many violent thoughts." Amber bowed her head and pretended to pray. "Lord, help us control our anger and not hurt the other person's ex. Save us from assault and battery charges. We can't raise a baby from a jail cell, God."

"Amen! Save us, Lord!" I shouted and Amber faked a slaying in the spirit and fell out on the bed.

A'ndrea G. Wilson

Unlike my father, I was sure of where I wanted to be. There was no woman who could make me shine both inside and out like Amber could. I wanted to tell Amber more about Jay, but we were having such a good time that I didn't want to ruin our evening with all of the details. The conversation about Jay could wait until another time. We spent the rest of the evening talking and playing. I knew tomorrow had its challenges, but for tonight, my bride and I enjoyed laughter, intimacy, and friendship.

Lesson 19: Thy Will Be Done

Many plans are in a man's mind, but it is the Lord's purpose for him that will stand. (Proverbs 19:21)

Amber and I sat in my car the next morning. I closed my eyes, trying to build the courage to get out and face the legal process of getting joint custody of Jonelle. I was more nervous than I thought I would be. The immediate fate of my child's placement was in the hands of a judge, and the mere thought of it made me feel like throwing up. Now, I knew why I had never pressed the issue of custody in the past; I didn't want to have to go through the court system. I was afraid that somehow the state would find a reason to label me as an unfit parent and make it difficult for me to be with my child. Because of this underlying fear, I had played the game by Lena's rules, keeping the law out of the picture and thinking it would earn me a position closer to my daughter. Well, I had been wrong. Regardless of my attempts to pacify Lena, my child had constantly been kept from me. Placing the matter in the hands of the justice system was my only hope of providing my daughter with a childhood that reflected a continuous father presence. My father wasn't perfect, but he was there, and I desperately needed to be there for Jonelle, just as my dad had been there for me.

Amber, noticing my apprehension, grabbed my hand and caressed it. "Baby, it's gonna be okay."

I opened my eyes and offered her a weak smile. "I hope so."

"How about we pray before we go in there? Maybe that will help soothe some of your nerves."

I took a deep breath in and let it out. "Yeah, cool. I could use all the prayer I can get right now."

We both bowed our heads and closed our eyes. Amber led the prayer. "God, You know the battle that we face today and the lives that are on the line. Go before us and make a way, despite any obstacle that stands in our path. We know that family is Your creation and that Jonelle needs both her mother and her father. We have our own plans, God, but let Your will be done. In Jesus' name we pray, Amen."

"Amen."

She squeezed my hand and motioned for us to get moving. Taking in one last deep breath, I exited the vehicle and started toward the courthouse.

My attorney, Ms. Sherri Greene, was waiting for us in the hallway when we walked into the building. She appeared very "official" in her black pantsuit and rectangle-shaped, black-rimmed eyeglasses, which made me feel slightly more at ease. She had defended cases like mine a million times; everything would be fine.

After greeting us and going over a few minor details, she led us into our assigned courtroom where another case was currently being presented. I looked around the room and didn't see Lena or Jonelle, but a few minutes later, they entered through the double doors along with two men. One of the men seemed very comfortable with Lena, for he kept his hand on her back during their entrance and sat extremely close to her on the bench. *Was this some new boyfriend of hers? I* didn't care if she was dating, but why would she bring this guy to our custody hearing?

Our case was called thirty minutes later. Ms. Greene introduced me and Amber as the ideal couple: newlyweds, business owners, upper class, and stable. All we wanted was the opportunity to share custody with the child's mother.

Lena's attorney, a man named Mr. Kevin Deere, attempted to paint a different story. Lena was a hard-working, single mother who had been abandoned by the father of her child. Since then, the father had been harassing her, unwilling to support the child adequately and attempting to control Lena.

I shook my head at the lies and shenanigans. It was typical, manipulative Lena, but the sucker punch was her attorney making two claims: the mystery man was Lena's fiancé, and they were requesting additional time to provide evidence that would prove Lena's concerns about Jonelle's well-being if I were given joint custody.

Mr. Deere's words hit me fast and hard like two, cold snowballs to the face. *Lena's fiancé? Concerns about Jonelle's well-being.* I glanced over at Lena who was playing the role like an Academy Award winning actress. She clutched the mystery man-slash-fiancé's arm and cowered over as if she was intimidated by the whole scenario. The man, as if on cue, wrapped one big arm around her body and rocked her like they were at a funeral rather than in family court. I guess Amber was also watching the scene because she elbowed me and mumbled, "I can't stand her," under her breath.

It didn't bother me that Lena was so-called engaged. It just seemed mighty convenient that her engagement was being publically announced at our custody hearing. I honestly didn't believe it was true. Knowing her, she probably suckered the guy into agreeing to come with her to make her case stronger, especially because I had the benefit of being married. I secretly hoped she would get married. Then she might stop worrying so much about my marriage. My biggest apprehension about her new beau was his presence around and effect on my child.

And what was this whole accusation of me being a threat to my daughter's well-being? Only Lena could find a way to convince a courtroom of people that a responsible man who actually wanted to be a father to his daughter was harmful to the child. I clinched my teeth to refrain from saying or doing anything that would make me look "unsafe," as she was suggesting.

Both attorneys were called to the bench, and when they returned, the judge was pounding his gavel and dismissing us from the courtroom.

"What happened?" I frantically asked Ms. Greene as she ushered us out of the room.

She walked us down the hall a bit, giving us privacy from others standing nearby. "Basically, they are claiming they need more time to build their case, so the judge has granted them an additional two weeks. In the meantime, you will have weekend visitation with Jonelle and Thanksgiving. Lena is ordered to bring Jonelle to you for these visitations. You'll have to return to court on November 30th where they will have to show valid proof of why you shouldn't be allowed joint custody. If they cannot do so at that time, the judge is likely to rule in your favor."

I let out a sigh of relief. "That's good news, right?"

Ms. Greene smiled. "Yes, it is. You don't have a criminal record or anything that would hurt your case. You are all caught up on child support payments, so I would say that unless they can work magic and pull a rabbit out of a hat, Lena doesn't have a case against you. But I have to warn you. With the exception of picking up Jonelle and dropping her off for the weekend, maintain limited contact with Lena. She may not have anything now, but might be trying to trick you into doing something that would ruin your chances. Don't give her any ammunition."

Amber and I both nodded in agreement. We understood that we were at war, and all was fair in love and war.

I was thrilled when Jonelle came to stay with us that following weekend. I hadn't spent any time with my daughter in months; being close to her felt better than ever. Lena dropped her off on Friday evening. I could see the irritated look on her face as she drove away, but she was smart enough to know not to go against the ruling of the judge.

Jonelle had her own room in our house. It was one of the things that Amber and I had decided when we got married, that Jonelle should have a room that belonged to her to make her feel just as much of a part of our family as she felt at home with her mother. We let Jonelle help us pick out her furniture, toys, and decorations to make it feel uniquely hers. When she wasn't with us, we agreed not to allow others to go into her room so that when she returned, it would be just as she had left it. Giving her a space to call her own helped Jonelle quickly to feel comfortable after weeks or months of being away from us.

We spent the weekend watching movies, going bowling, making pizza and ice cream sundaes, and shopping for food for Thanksgiving dinner, which was the next week. We finished the weekend off by attending my church as a family so that my parents and siblings could see Jonelle. When Jonelle was kept from me, she was also kept from all of us. That's what Lena couldn't understand: not only was she depriving Jonelle of building a relationship with me, but also she was depriving her of her grandparents, aunts, uncles, and cousins as well. Everyone was excited to spend a little time with Jonelle, and we all agreed to have an early dinner at my parents' house to stretch the time out.

I was so caught up with enjoying my daughter that I completely disregarded my unresolved emotions toward my father. The friction remained between us, but I continued on as if everything was normal. We both barely got to be around Jonelle and I didn't want the affair drama to ruin the time she had with either of us.

By 4 PM, Amber and I were heading home with Jonelle. Lena was scheduled to pick her up at 5 o'clock, and the last thing we wanted to do was not be there when she arrived. In the car on the way home, I decided to ask Jonelle about her mother's new man.

"So your mom is getting married. You OK with that?"

Amber peered at me, her facial expression indicating she was surprised I was bringing up the issue.

Jonelle shrugged her shoulders. "I guess. I don't know."

"You don't know? Do you *like* . . . what's his name?"

"His name is Phillip. He's all right. He's been coming around for a while, but she always acted as if she didn't want to be bothered with him. He's nice to me, though. He always brings me candy bars."

It was just as I thought. Lena was using this guy. I looked over at Amber who twisted her lips, obviously reading my mind. I decided to change the conversation at that point. I didn't want to pull Jonelle into the middle of our adult squabbles any more than she already was. We spent the remainder of the ride talking about what she wanted for Christmas.

Lena was at my door at 4:59. I hugged and kissed Jonelle before sending her away with her mother. Lena flicked me a half of a goodbye wave and rushed Jonelle to the car. It's amazing how someone that I spent so much time with and had created a baby with could turn so cold and callous toward me. I wasn't sure exactly what I had done to Lena, or when I had done it, but in her mind, I was the devil himself. I can honestly say that I tried to make things work between her and me. I never wanted to have a child out of wedlock or not be in the same home as my kid. Despite our differences, I really cared about Lena when we were together, but at the time, we were starting to hate each other, so I thought it would be best to end the relationship before one of us killed the other. From the fleeing, evil scowl Lena gave me as she got into her car, killing me was still a very real option for her. The tires on her car screeched as she abruptly pulled away from the curb. *Yep, if given the chance, she would definitely kill me.*

Lesson 20: It's Time To Man-Up

When I was a child, I talked like a child, I thought like a child, I reasoned like a child; now that I have become a man, I am done with childish ways and have put them aside. (I Corinthians 13:11)

Martin gathered his Bible in his arms and said, "Moving on to I Corinthians 13:11, 'When I was a child, I talked like a child, I thought like a child, I reasoned like a child; now that I have become a man, I am done with childish ways and have put them aside.' I'm certain most of you have either read or heard of this verse before, but I wonder how many times you have heard it as it relates to love and loving others. Probably none of you have heard it in this context."

I was still feeling the high from my weekend with the family. It felt so good to have my wife, my daughter, and my relatives all in one place, enjoying each other's company. Now more than ever, I needed to gain joint custody of Jonelle. I wanted every weekend to be like the one that had just passed: me, Amber, Jonelle, and soon, the new baby too. As much as I enjoyed working and fulfilling my career goals, at the end of the day I was doing it all so that I could be a better provider for my family. I was starting to comprehend that my family was more important than any amount of success I could gain, even the kind of success that came from White House parties.

"It is somewhat easy to think of being a child when it comes to immaturity in other areas of our lives, but let's focus on how a man can be mature or immature in his loving," Martin continued. "The verse comes at us as if Apostle Paul is talking about himself. He is telling us that there are some behaviors that he demonstrated as a child, some words he said as a child, some thoughts he thought as a child, and some rationale that he had as a child that no longer make sense to his adult self. Now that he has 'matured' into a man, for him to continue moving forward in his manhood, he must put aside childish ways.

"This verse serves not to reveal to us something about Paul, but to show us something about ourselves. Some of us want to call ourselves men, but we are still operating as a child would. We are still having immature words come out of our mouths, actions being displayed, thoughts circling our minds, and reasoning to explain the world around us. If we want to be considered as men, we must put aside these childish ways and embrace the words, actions, thoughts, and rationale of men."

Martin laid his Bible down on the podium. "Verse eleven comes after the verses discussing the imperfect being made perfect. This leads me to believe that childishness is compared to imperfection and manhood is compared to completeness or perfection. It's OK to make mistakes and errors that hurt others when we are children; we don't know any better. But when we are adults, when we are men and are still hurting others despite the fact that we now know better, it is no longer acceptable. God is here and He is providing us the opportunity to love as He loves, but we are still being childish. Men, it's time to grow up. It's time to man-up. It's time to stop being selfish and self-centered. It's time to operate in the spirit of love. When someone acts rudely to you, treat them with kindness anyways. You're a grown man;

you don't play tit-for-tat like a child anymore. When someone does you dirty, forgive them and forget about it. You're a man; you don't keep records of the wrong done against you like a child would. Grow up. If you want to call yourself a man, it's time to act like one. Man-up, Brothers, man-up."

Martin was on point. It was time for me to put childish ways behind me and be the man that God had created me to be. It was time for me to let go of any resentment toward my father about his fling that happened forty plus years ago. It was time for me to deal with Lena like a man and not feed into her petty behavior. It was time for me to put Jay in her place and end all of the unproductive flirtation and advances. Who cared if I lost a few big accounts? I would win so much more by having peace in my heart and in my mind. Amber and I weren't hurting financially in the least bit, so why was I stressing over a few dollars. Yes, I wanted to experience the elation of achievement, but not if it was attached to compromising myself and my values. I might have lost myself and my head for a little while, but as I climbed into my sparkling-clean Caddy that evening, I smiled, knowing the real Eric Hayes was back and ready to reclaim my life.

One problem: *Why is it so easy to get in trouble, yet difficult to get out of it?*

Lesson 21: Exit, Stage Right

And I found that [of all sinful follies none has been so ruinous in seducing one away from God as idolatrous women] more bitter than death is the woman whose heart is snares and nets and whose hands are bands. Whoever pleases God shall escape from her, but the sinner shall be taken by her. (Ecclesiastes 7:26)

It was the Wednesday before Thanksgiving, and I was trying to wrap up a few business items so that I could enjoy my four-day weekend. I had given the realty's agents an option to take the day off if they needed to travel for the holiday, so only a few of us remained around the office. Workday or not, I told Amber I would be home by 3 o'clock. She was at the house, getting help from Tisha on how to cook cornbread dressing and collard greens. It was our first Thanksgiving as a married couple; we wanted to make it special. Instead of gathering with the rest of my family or going up north to visit hers, we agreed to stay at home and celebrate the day in our own house. Psyched that Jonelle would be there with us, we had planned a weekend of eating, Black Friday shopping, and relaxing.

Around one o'clock, I got a call from the bank, informing me of Jay's closing date in four weeks. It had taken a little longer than expected to pull their side of the deal together, but in a month, right before Christmas, Jay would be the owner of another building, and I would get a big, fat commission check. Although I was no longer enthralled with the financial gain of the sell, it was nice to know that all of my hard work was going to pay off. I phoned Jay to tell her the good news.

"That's just what I needed to hear!" she shrieked. "It was starting to feel like this thing was never going to happen. Please remind me to never again by a property that is facing foreclosure."

I wouldn't be reminding Jay of anything. As far as I was concerned, this was my first and last business deal with her. Of course, I couldn't say that to her. "Well, you're getting a great deal, so it's probably worth the slight delay."

"Yeah, you're right," she replied. "Listen, I'm going out-of-town for a couple of weeks, but don't worry, I'll be back in time for the closing. I have a few kinks I need to work out at my Los Angeles location. I swear my job is never done. Anyways, can you meet me at ESPN Zone in Buckhead in an hour?"

Meet her at ESPN Zone? No way. I was going home to my wife. "I can't. Why?"

"To celebrate! We *have* got to have one toast before I leave tonight!"

Nope. The last thing I needed to do was to be out with her. "I really can't. I'm supposed to be–"

"Eric, it's just a quick toast. I promise! It's a good luck ritual I do every time I'm getting ready to close on a building. Call any of my past real estate agents, and they'll tell you. They all had to have one toast. If it makes you feel any better, my flight leaves at six so I don't have much time to linger. Pleeeaaase!"

I gritted my teeth. My plan was to wash my hands of this woman, but somehow I couldn't get rid of her. Maybe this was just what I needed, to meet with her and set the record straight: I was NOT interested. She wasn't going to back off until I made it painfully obvious that there would never be a romantic relationship between us. With the intentions of seeing her to put her in check, I said, "OK. One toast and I have to leave. Meet me there at 2:30."

When I got to ESPN Zone, Jay was already there and had made herself comfortable in a crescent-shaped booth in front of the theater-size TV screen. I dryly greeted her and slid into the booth, praying I could get this whole toast and truth scene done and over with quickly.

"I ordered some wine. Did you want anything else?" she asked, her tone optimistic as usual.

"No, I'm good."

The screen in front of us was showing highlights from Sunday and Monday's games. Due to the past weekend's festivities and Monday's class, I had missed the majority of the recent football games; I couldn't help but to watch was happening on the large TV. Before I knew it, the waiter was bringing a bottle of overpriced wine and two glasses. Once the wine had been poured and the waiter had retreated, Jay pushed my glass over to me, raised hers, and proceeded in her salute. "To dreams come true! Cheers!"

I unenthusiastically lifted my glass, clunked it against hers, and took a sip of the bitter liquid. I had no intentions of finishing the wine; I didn't even like the taste of it anyway. Now that the toast was over, I planned to make our nonexistent relationship clear, and roll out. "Thanks for the toast, Jay. I need to be leaving," I started.

"But you just got here. Finish your wine first," she whined.

"Jay, I can't do this with you. I am flattered by your interest in me, but as I've told you before, I'm married, and I love my wife. I really appreciate all that you've done for me, but you have got to respect my boundaries. Now, I–"

I was going to say that I had to leave to get home to my wife, but before I could complete my sentence, Jay lunged at me and attacked my lips with hers. She ran her tongue across the opening of my mouth then proceeded to suck on my lower lip as if it were a ripe grape. The kiss lasted all of six seconds before I was able to push her away and reclaim my mouth.

"What are you doing?" I roared, as I wiped my mouth with the back of my hand.

"Stop fighting this, Eric. We could be good together," she pleaded.

"You're delusional!" I pulled several dollars out of my wallet to pay for my unconsumed glass of wine, tossed them on the table, and stormed away. I heard Jay screaming my name as I left, but I refused to look back. I should have never agreed to meet her. It was just another trap, another set up to reel me in. Jay had not been lying when she said that she didn't accept the word no.

By the time I fought through holiday traffic and got home, Jonelle was already there and Tisha was getting ready to leave. I didn't want to seem as frustrated as I really felt because I didn't want Amber asking me questions, so I plastered on a happy grin as I walked through the door.

"Oh man! It smells great in here!" I exclaimed as I entered the kitchen. Amber was sitting at the kitchen table with Jonelle, cutting cookie dough into Thanksgiving shapes like leaves and pilgrims. Tisha was sliding her jacket on and giving Amber reminders about warming up the food tomorrow.

"Hey babe," Amber replied to me. "Give Tisha the credit because my feet are too swollen to do anything today. She had to hook us up."

I walked over to Amber and Jonelle and gave them both kisses on the forehead. "Thanks, Tisha! You're a lifesaver," I said while moving over to her and pulling her into a friendly hug.

"Get off of me!" she joked. "Your wife set me up! I'm not fooling with you two anymore. I still have to go to my own house and cook for those greedy relatives of mine!"

Tisha gave us both an evil glare before rolling her eyes and heading out the door.

Amber and I laughed at Tisha's antics, knowing she would be back to help with Christmas dinner. Amber wasn't the best cook, but she was slowly learning with the guidance of Tisha and Nessy. Before Amber and I dated, she rarely cooked, but after taking the Wife 101 class, she started making efforts to become better with domestic activities. It would take some time, and she probably would never turn into Betty Crocker, but I appreciated her willingness to try.

The holiday weekend went by without a hitch. We had a quiet Thanksgiving at home filled with great food and a bunch of family movies. On Black Friday, we woke up at 4 in the morning to catch the early bird specials that began at 5 AM at the mall. It was a challenge, yet fun, to plot and plan with Amber to buy Christmas gifts for Jonelle without her seeing them. We would take turns making excuses to leave the group, buy something, and then stuff it into the trunk before catching back up with the other two. We spent Saturday over my parents' house and Sunday morning at Amber's church. I hated to see Jonelle leave on Sunday afternoon. Our next court date was on Friday, and I hoped it would be the last. If the judged ruled in favor of joint custody, I would be spending a lot more weekends with my baby girl. Amber and I felt confident that we would win in court, but we sent up a prayer every night, just in case.

Lesson 22: Once Was Blind But Now I See

For now we are looking in a mirror that gives only a dim (blurred) reflection [of reality as in a riddle or enigma], but then [when perfection comes] we shall see in reality and face to face! Now I know in part (imperfectly), but then I shall know and understand fully and clearly, even in the same manner as I have been fully and clearly known and understood [by God]. (I Corinthians 13:12)

By Monday evening, my nerves were shot. I didn't know why, but the pending court decision was causing me to feel anxious. All the "what ifs" filled my head. *What if they rule against me? What if Lena concocts some ridiculous lie about me? What if the judge stereotypes me as a deadbeat dad? What if they increase my child support payments? What if I oversleep and miss the hearing? What if Jonelle tells the judge she doesn't want to spend more time with me?* The enemy was certainly playing games with my mind. I looked forward to the Husband 101 class as a mental distraction and a spiritual shield against my negative thinking.

As usual, Martin took control of the class by directing us to the Word. "We are up to I Corinthians 13:12. And it reads, 'For now we are looking in a mirror that gives only a dim, blurred, reflection, of reality as in a riddle or enigma, but then, when perfection comes, we shall see in reality and face to face! Now I know in part, imperfectly, but then I shall know and understand fully and clearly, even in the same manner as I have been fully and clearly known and understood, by God.'

"Brothers, we are still studying love. If we go back in our lessons, you will remember me teaching that God is love, and His love can reside in us, or it could be said that He can reside in us. We often talk about God living in us as the Holy Spirit or Holy Ghost. Regardless what name you use to identify God's power, presence and love living in you, He is there if you have received Him. Jesus tells us that He waits for us. He says that He stands at the door to your heart and knocks, waiting to be invited in and abide with you."

"Amen," I said, along with a few other members of the class.

"In our natural state, our lives are dim and our reflections are blurry. Have you ever tried to look into a mirror that was dirty or broken or even foggy? If so, you will know that it is difficult to see your entire face in a mirror that is flawed or imperfect. Even if the mirror is bent, the reflection you get will be skewed, sort of like walking through a carnival's House of Mirrors. Everything looks off, weird, even funny. Without God's perfection, without His love in us, an incomplete picture is all that we are and all that we reflect."

Martin paced the front of the room. "Have you ever noticed that the main people who mope around, claiming that they have no idea of who they are or what they are supposed to be are usually those who are distant from God? People who don't work on developing their relationship with God often struggle with their purpose because they are incomplete and only reflect part of who they were created to be. This is why it is so important that we not only ask for salvation, but nurture or 'work out' that salvation in us. We cannot afford to stop at salvation; we must continue onward to decreasing in self so that He can increase in our lives. This is the only way we can get in touch with who we are, by being close to the one who made us.

"In verse twelve, we are encouraged to grow in the perfection of God, to allow Him to have His way. He is able to bring us to a place of true reality, fully and clearly understanding who we are. The problem is not that God doesn't know us; it's that we don't know ourselves. We cannot see ourselves nor understand ourselves because we are looking through a faulty mirror." Martin chuckled to himself. "I used to wonder why God loved me so much that He would give His Son for me. Many Christians wonder the same thing. But one of the reasons we don't understand why is because we don't know who we really are. We cannot fully see ourselves the way He sees us. It's like a parent looking at his child and knowing all the wonderful things that the child possesses. That child may make mistakes and disappoint his father, but the father loves him anyway because the father sees and knows that child better than the child sees and knows himself. One day, that child will grow up and come into the full knowledge of all that he is, and then he will be able to understand his father's love."

Martin stopped pacing and looked out at us. "The same is true for us. God loves us despite our mistakes because He knows exactly what He created. He also knows what happens when we allow love to have its perfect way. He is able to show us the real us. It reminds me of the hymn 'Amazing Grace' and its lyrics, 'I once was lost, but now I'm found, was blind, but now I see.' Let's take a few minutes to sing that song together."

At Martin's cue we all began to sing the popular, gospel hymn. "Amazing Grace, how sweet the sound, that saved a wretch like me. . ."

I drove home that night in silence. I could still hear the melody to the song ringing in my ears. It was God's grace that was removing the blinders from my eyes and revealing to me all that a husband and a man should be. I was beginning to realize that all of the trials I was experiencing were developing my character as a man. Every issue was aimed at asking me vital questions about who I was and what I stood for. Would I fight for my family? Would I leave my child behind? Would I compromise my vows? Would I let pride tear down my home? Would I allow resentment and disappointment to keep me from being close to those I love? Would I walk in truth and faith or lies and fear? What did I value, and what did I treasure? Did I really love my wife, and would I sacrifice myself for her?

The questions were real and being asked. My answers were not about what I said, but about what I did. The true demonstration of my manhood had just begun.

Lesson 23: What You Don't Know Can Hurt You

Pride goes before destruction, and a haughty spirit before a fall.
(Proverbs 16:18)

Amber and I sat quietly in the courtroom as several other cases were heard before ours. Lena was present with her phony fiancé, but Jonelle was not. I wondered if my little girl was at school; I was sure that was the reason Lena would claim for not bringing her. A part of me was glad that she wasn't there. I didn't want her to see her mother and father going back and forth to court over her. Yes, school was where she needed to be, not here. Lena had made a wise choice.

The one thing I could say in Lena's defense was that she was a decent mother to my child. Although we were no longer an item, I could trust her to care properly for my daughter. Jonelle never went without a hot meal, clothing, or shelter. I never worried if the electricity was cut off, or if Lena was using the child support money to get her hair and nails done, like other men I knew said about the mothers of their children. Honestly, the only issue that I had with Lena was her bitterness. As long as she got her way, everything was fine, but the minute I decided to not be in a relationship with her, the second I married someone else, the moment I went against what she wanted, her attitude and behavior toward me became spiteful and vindictive, always using Jonelle as her trump card. She knew that as long as she controlled Jonelle, she could control me because I would never do anything to put my child in harm's way. It was a classic story shared by many nonresidential fathers; I wasn't the first, and I wouldn't be the last man to deal with a bitter woman. What many of these women failed to realize was that the ones who suffered the most were not the fathers that they blamed for everything; it was the very children they claimed to love so much. So on this day, I was standing up to Lena for the sake of my daughter, to make sure she would never have to say that she grew up without a father in her life, modeling to her how a man should to treat a woman.

I glanced over at Lena who turned her head, looked back at me, and gave me a devious smile. She didn't seem as anxious or ruffled as I was feeling, which caused me to feel even more uneasy. It was obvious that she knew something that I didn't. She had a secret, one that would probably scar me, and there was nothing I could do but wait for her to play her hand. Or maybe it was just a poker face. Twenty minutes later, I would find out that the saying, "what you don't know won't hurt you," was a lie from the pit of Hell. What you don't know can nearly destroy you.

"Your honor, we have evidence that the child's father is not the upstanding citizen he claims to be." Lena's attorney, Mr. Deere, began his presentation to the judge.

My lawyer, Ms. Greene, peeked at me with an expressionless face, but I knew what she was thinking. "What is he talking about?" was really what she wanted to say. I offered her a subtle shrug to answer her unasked question.

Amber wrapped her fingers around my hand in support. I didn't dare look at her for fear she would be wondering the same thing as Ms. Greene.

I could feel Lena's eyes burning a hole into the side of my head. She wanted to see the look on my face when whatever she had up her sleeve was publicized. I promised myself I wouldn't give her that kind of satisfaction. Whatever it was, I wouldn't let her see my emotions. She would not get the best of me.

I quickly allowed my life to flash through my mind. I couldn't think of anything she could have on me. I wasn't perfect, but I had good ethics and morals. What could she prove about me that was so bad?

Mr. Deere pulled out of his briefcase a manila envelope. "I have here Exhibit A." He opened the envelope and pulled out a stack of letter-sized photographs. "These photographs show Mr. Hayes at various places around the city with a woman who is not his wife. In several of the photographs, he is seen kissing the woman in question."

The envelope contained a few sets of the photos. He provided one set to the judge and another to my attorney. As Ms. Greene and the judge flipped through the photos, Amber and I huddled up close to her to see them ourselves. I didn't know how Lena had done it, but she obviously had someone following me, taking pictures of my meetings with Jacqueline Johnson. There were pictures of us at every building viewing, at the all-white party, in her cars, and more recently at ESPN Zone.

I frantically whispered to Ms. Greene, "She's trying to frame me! That woman is a client of mine! There's nothing going on between us!" The pictures, however, told a different story. One photo was of Jay kissing me on the cheek inside her Maybach the night of the party. Another picture caught her kissing me at ESPN Zone, but it appeared as if I was returning the kiss.

I felt Amber's hand let go of mine, and in that moment, I became aware that not only was my custody of Jonelle at risk, so was my marriage.

I turned towards Amber. "Don't believe it!" I pleaded. "You know me. You know I wouldn't."

In the midst of the excitement, the judge finished shuffling through the photos and said, "Ms. Greene, do you have anything to say about this new evidence."

Ms. Greene composed herself and stood up, businesslike. "I was not aware of these photos, Your Honor; however, my client reports that this woman is a client of his business and that these pictures have been skewed to make their relationship appear as something it is not."

"Your Honor, we assumed that Mr. Hayes would deny the photos," Mr. Deere countered. "We have taken the liberty of inviting the woman in question to this hearing to verify her relationship with Mr. Hayes."

Someone stood up in the back of the room. I whipped my head around to see Jay making her way down the aisle. She stopped next to Mr. Deere. A hush fell over the courtroom.

"This woman is Jacqueline Johnson, and she is the woman in the photographs you are holding."

"Counselor Deere," the judge said. "This is very unorthodox. Do you understand that this is family court not criminal or civil court?"

"Yes, I do. I felt it was only fair to demonstrate the character of Mr. Hayes before a decision to release his daughter into his custody was granted."

"Very well. Counselors, I will not make a circus out of my courtroom so I will speak with Ms. Johnson privately in my chambers. I am scheduling another hearing for December 12. At that time I will rule on this case. Until that time, weekend visitation will be suspended, and Counselor Greene will be allowed to submit any material that challenges this adulterous claim." The judge banged his gavel and court was adjourned.

My eyes had never left Jay. She must have felt me gaping at her because she finally turned her head toward me and acknowledged my presence. I saw the edges of her mouth curl into a barely noticeable smile. She then shifted her eyes to Lena who was beaming in delight. Finally she glanced at Amber who was stoic, yet still by my side. A bailiff ended our eye war by escorting Jay to the judge's chamber.

Lena laughed, licked her index finger, and made an imaginary checkmark in the air, symbolizing that she had won. I had no time to dwell on her actions because Ms. Greene was discreetly shoving me out of the room. Amber followed, but I could tell by her demeanor that she was seconds away from exploding.

"What in the world happened in there?" Ms. Greene said once we were finally alone. "I'll tell you what happened. The mother of your child caught you with your pants down!"

Flustered, I threw my hands up in the air. "I swear I never touched that woman. She kept coming on to me. She kissed me! I told her that I was married, but she wouldn't stop. That picture is a lie! She kissed me; it doesn't show the full story! I pushed her away and ran out of the room! I can't believe this! This is bogus!"

Ms. Greene scratched her head and directed her attention to Amber. "Did you know anything about this, Mrs. Hayes?"

"Eric did mention that one of his clients was interested in him," Amber said stiffly before lowering her eyes to the ground.

It was crucial that I proved my innocence, but who or what could save me? *Carl!* "I also have an employee, Carl Fenton, who knows this woman has been trying to get at me," I shouted. "Why didn't I listen to him and let him handle her account?"

Ms. Greene pulled out her cell phone. "OK. Calm down. Get me Mr. Fenton's number, and I will do everything I can to straighten this out. Call me if you can think of any other witnesses or ways to disprove these photos." She dialed her assistant's number, and when the woman answered the phone, she said, "Kay, it's Sherri. I need you to do some digging for me." She gestured that she would be in touch and began to speed walk away.

The drive home was a silent one. I waited for Amber to say something, but she didn't which was extremely out of character for her. Amber was the type to rant and rave; she never had learned how to hold her tongue. The fact that she managed to get all of the way back to the house without saying a word let me know that I was getting ready to see a side of her that I had never seen before (and never wanted to see again).

The minute I put the car in park, she jumped out of the passenger seat and flew inside the house. I took in a deep breath, preparing myself for the worst, as I followed her into our home. I found her sitting in her favorite spot on the sofa in the living room, staring out of the huge bay window.

"Are you going to talk to me?" I asked, gearing up for my punishment.

She tore her eyes away from the window and glared at me. "The problem isn't me not talking to you; it's you not talking to me. My tolerance is low, and I really don't feel like being around you right now, so you better start explaining fast."

I took a seat across from her and proceeded to tell her everything from Carl warning me about Jay to our last meeting at ESPN Zone. I even told her about the all-white party and me moving the ring.

"Amber, I wanted to tell you the truth, but at the same time, I wanted this deal so badly. I just wanted you to see that I could grow your business."

Her mouth dropped open. "My business? Eric, it is YOUR business. It's been YOUR business ever since we got married. Why don't you get that? You don't have to prove anything to me!"

I shook my head in disagreement. "You say that, but I feel like if I fail, if this business falls apart, then I will be the one to blame for ruining your first company. I just don't want to let you down."

"So now it's my fault because I tried to set my husband up with a good career so that he wouldn't have to start at the bottom. Am I the one to blame for all of this?"

"No, Amber. It's not your fault."

She stood up and moved closer to me. "Then tell me why you felt the need to lie to me! That's what hurts the most; that you withheld the truth from me . . . I know a scandalous woman when I see one! Like a typical male, you just don't know the difference. Jacqueline Johnson is a low-class Jezebel! But you let her trick you, and now you might not get custody of your daughter because of it." She released a heavy sigh. "So all of this time, your male client Jay has really been your female client Jay?"

I lowered my eyes to the floor in shame. "Yes."

"Umm Um. See, that's what I am talking about! You knew I thought Jay was a man, and you never corrected me. You know that makes you look guilty, right?"

My eyes widened as I looked up at her. "I know, but I swear I'm not! I love you; I wouldn't cheat on you. I know I should have handled the situation differently, and now it has all blown up in my face. I'm so sorry, Amber. Please tell me what I need to do to make all of this right?"

She placed her right hand on her hip. "Oh, *now* you want my advice? There is nothing you can do except lie in the bed you made. Take your whooping like a man, Eric. It's done."

I was waiting for her to tell me that she wanted a divorce, that our marriage was over, but she didn't. "So you're not going to leave me?"

"Don't tempt me, Eric! No, I'm not leaving you, but right now, I can't stand to look at your face so I suggest you go somewhere."

I exhaled in relief. "OK, but babe—"

"Eric, you've got about five seconds to get out of my face before I change my mind."

I nodded, took one last look at her, and headed back out the door. I got into my car and drove to the only other place that I felt completely safe in Metro Atlanta, my parents' house, of course. I was ashamed of what I had done and the mess that I had put my family in. I really didn't want to have to admit my faults to my parents, especially my father after I had just been so judgmental toward him, but sooner or later they would hear about it anyway. I would rather the truth come from my lips.

Both of my parents, along with my brother Nelson were in the garage, pulling out Christmas decorations. They remembered that I had my court hearing that day, so the moment they saw me, they instantly knew something had gone wrong. They all stopped fooling with the numerous boxes labeled HOLIDAYS and directed their attention at me, waiting in anticipation for me to deliver the bad news.

"Hey," I said, apprehensively.

"Oh no," my mother replied. "What happened?"

I ran my hand down the back of my neck. "I'm still not really sure what happened or how it happened, but Lena ambushed me. She must have had someone following me. Whoever it was took a bunch of pictures of me with one of my clients, a woman. The pictures made it seem as if I was having affair, but I wasn't. I'm not!"

"Oh Lord!" my mother cried out.

My father dropped the string of lights that remained in his hand. Nelson smirked.

"I have to go back to court in two weeks," I continued. "The judge will rule on the case then."

"And Amber?" my mother asked.

"She's upset, and she has every right to be. I told her about a client who had showed interest in me, but I didn't tell her everything. I basically lied to her. I feel awful about it."

Nelson took several steps toward me and patted me on the back. Just when I thought he had matured and was going to offer some support and brotherly comfort, he said, "Well, if she divorces you, you can probably keep the Cadillac and the business since they are both in your name."

My father grunted and responded, "Nelson, if you're not going to be helpful, take your skinny behind home. Matter of fact, go on. You're starting to get on my nerves anyway."

Nelson looked offended. "Oh so that's how it is? The Golden Child Eric is running around town with some woman, and I'm the one who has to go home? All right, all right. I'm leaving. Let Eric help you put up the Christmas tree since y'all love him so much." Nelson began to walk out of the garage, but turned around and said, "E, man. I told you. It was only a matter of time before it all came down on your head.

I knew it was going to fall apart. It's gravity, baby! But nobody wants to listen to Nelson."

My father stepped toward Nelson. "Boy, don't make me have to–"

Nelson raised his hands in surrender. "I'm leaving!" he said before exiting the garage, getting into his car, and pulling out of the driveway.

My mother came over to me and began to hug me.

"So what are you going to do?" my dad asked.

With my mom's arms still wrapped around me, I said, "I'm not sure. I really think that I need to talk to this woman, make her tell the truth so that I can still get custody of my child."

My mom backed away from me. "What does she have to do with Jonelle?"

"She was there at court. I don't know if she's in on it or if they just found her and got her to go along with their plan. Either way, because of her, I might not win my case."

"Now, Son, don't go making this thing worse than it already is."

"I have to do something, Dad. I can't just sit back and let Lena and this woman, Jacqueline, ruin my family."

My father sighed. "I understand. Do what you have to do, but before you do anything stupid, make sure to discuss it with The Man Above."

I had heard my father's advice to me, but I still couldn't shake the urge to try to talk some sense into Jay. I sat in my car, in my parents' driveway, staring at my cell phone, debating if I should call her. I didn't want to complicate matters, but I had to know if she was a part of this elaborate scheme all along. *But seriously, who does that? Who buys a building just to con someone?* It didn't make sense.

Needing to know the truth, I scrolled through my contact list and pressed SEND on her phone number. After three rings, she answered.

"I'm surprised that it has taken you this long to call me. I was certain you would call right after you left court," she said, her voice upbeat and confident.

"So you wanted this? You set this up? Jay, what's going on?"

She laughed, but I didn't think anything was funny. "Did I set this up? Not really. It just kind of worked out. I call it fate."

"What do you mean?" I asked, completely baffled.

"After you left me at ESPN Zone, I was angry, obviously. Then this guy comes up to me. Says he's a private investigator and that he's been following you for a while. He had witnessed the whole show between us. I was ready to curse him out, but then I thought about it. He needed me to agree to testify in court, and I needed your marriage to end. What better way for everyone to get what they wanted? I'm sure after that whole scene today your wife is through with you, so now we can be together. Isn't that what you want?"

I had allowed myself to become entangled in a fool's web. Only on TV had I ever heard of someone being so irrational. This woman was certifiably crazy. "What? Are you insane? Do you hear yourself? You don't seem to get it, so let me make it crystal clear. I don't want you! I love my wife! There is NO us! Stop trying to force me to be with you because it's never going to happen."

She huffed. "Fine! Well then you'll never get custody of your daughter. Isn't that what this whole court mess was all about? Eric, I can help you get her back. I can talk to the judge, but you've got to be reasonable and let this wife thing go."

I was livid. Did she really believe that she could continue to bait me? "Wow! I can't believe that a woman, who has so much to offer, has such a low self-esteem. Why would you want to be with a man that doesn't want you? If you stopped trying to manipulate married men, you might find a single one who actually likes you. I'm going to tell you like this. I don't need your help to get my daughter back."

She had the audacity to get indignant. "We will see about that! Good luck with trying to explain that kiss to your wife. And I'm going to tell you like this. I'm pulling out of our contract!"

I hung up the phone. I couldn't take the sound of her voice anymore. Who cared if she pulled out of the contract? The money wasn't worth the headache.

Feeling overwhelmed and outnumbered, I finally took my father's advice and prayed. "God, I know I've made too many mistakes to count, and I know I put my own self in this situation, but I believe You still can rescue my family from this pit. Please give me favor with the judge and let him grant custody of my daughter to me. Please reconcile my marriage and help Amber to trust me again. And please forgive me for not being obedient and loving my wife with Your love. Teach me how to love her as I love myself and be willing to sacrifice myself for her. I truly desire to be the man you created me to be. In Jesus' name, amen."

I started the car and drove home. Not surprisingly, I slept in the guest room that night and the next.

Lesson 24: The Greatest Gift Is Love

And so faith, hope, love abide [faith—conviction and belief respecting man's relation to God and divine things; hope—joyful and confident expectation of eternal salvation; love—true affection for God and man, growing out of God's love for us and in us], these three; but the greatest of these is love. (I Corinthians 13:13)

"We have only three classes left including today's lesson," Martin stated. "We have come to the final verse in I Corinthians 13. Let's turn to the thirteenth verse and see how the chapter ends. 'And so faith, hope, love abide, faith, conviction and belief respecting man's relation to God and divine things; hope, joyful and confident expectation of eternal salvation; love, true affection for God and man, growing out of God's love for us and in us, these three; but the greatest of these is love.' "

The weekend had been a rough one for me. Returning to the Husband 101 class on Monday was necessary. Amber was barely speaking to me, and tiptoeing around her made me feel like a guest in my own home. At this point, my hands were tied, and there was nothing I could do about my marriage or Jonelle's custody case but wait to see what happened once the smoke cleared. I had come to the class praying that something Martin taught would help me get through the trials of my life.

Martin pointed at his Bible. "I just love the way the Amplified version provides a quick definition for faith, hope, and love. Faith is described as man's belief and conviction in God and divine things. Hope is described as joyful and confident expectation in eternity with God, and love is described as true affection for God and man that develops from God's love in and for us.

"Although all three of these characteristics are viewed as abiding or long lasting, the verse notifies us that love is actually the greatest out of them all. It's not surprising that love would be declared the greatest considering the fact that God is love, and He is the greatest of all. God desires for us to have faith and hope. Both of these traits are required in this life and to building a relationship with God, but even more so, He requires that we have love. He even goes as far as to ask us, how can we say that we love Him who we cannot see, but do not love those around us that we see every day? He commands us to love Him and love our neighbors, and He requires us to love our wives as Christ loves us. The word love is constantly tangled in God's instructions to us as people and as men."

Martin leaned against the podium. "There are a lot of things that we do for others, a lot of gifts that we give whether it's a physical present, a service, words, or some other form of giving. We often think we've done something major when we are able to give. We feel good about ourselves for our selflessness and thought, but, brothers, I tell you today that the greatest gift that anyone could ever receive is love. When people receive love, they receive God. Yes, receiving love is bringing people to God's salvation, but receiving love is also when people experience God's love through you. Every time you show your wife love, you are allowing her to feel the presence of God. Each time you share love with others, they get to know and see God through you. Loving people is powerful because God is revealed on this earth every time we choose to love. The next time you want to do something special for someone, love them; love them with God's love in you."

How many times had I heard the saying, "the greatest gift is love" and never truly considered what it really meant? I was guilty, like most men, of giving the people I cared about everything but my love. As a man, I often showed my affection through gifts and service to people. Yeah, I would buy my wife something new or fix a broken item for her, but how much did I give my love by being a reflection of God's presence? I thought about many of the times I felt God's presence in my life and many of the times God reminded me of how much He truly cared for me. His love wasn't felt as much when I received something new materialistically or through something big He made happen in my life as it was through the beautiful moments in life that mattered most, like when I gawked at nature early in the morning or when I held my wife in the middle of the night. Seeing my daughter smile at me or witnessing my parents kissing after almost fifty years of marriage, those were the times when God's love and presence were the strongest.

Rebuilding my relationship with my wife would not be easy. It would not come via flowers, dinners, or kind words. All of those things were nice gestures that I would do to ease the process, but the real healing would happen as I let God shine through me; only His love could mend her shattered trust. She needed to see a better me, one that was committed to God first, his family second, and everything else last. She had to know that I wouldn't hurt her because hurting her meant hurting myself. Like Martin had shown us in Corinthians, we were imperfect, I was imperfect, but that wasn't an excuse to be less of a man. With God living in me, He could clean up the ugliness inside of me if I would only let Him take over and use me. Many Christians spoke about being poured out vessels, but now I was starting to comprehend exactly what sacrifice was all about. Letting go. It could no longer be my way or my understanding; I had to let go and trust The Divine One. I had to remember that all things were working together for my good even when life appeared to be falling apart. I went home feeling more optimistic about my future and that of my family, but from experience I knew, to get to the mountaintop, I had a long way to climb.

Lesson 25: The Wages Of Sin Is Death

For the wages which sin pays is death, but the [bountiful] free gift of
God is eternal life through (in union with) Jesus Christ our Lord.

(Romans 6:23)

I pulled up to my house, confused by the sight of paramedics,
emergency vehicles, and flashing red and blue lights. Amber! My heart
beat wildly as I began to think of all of the atrocities that could have
happened to her. I jumped out of the car and rushed past the small
crowd of people and into the house. A uniformed police officer
grabbed me as I proceeded through the foyer, screaming out Amber's
name.

"This is my house!" I pleaded with the officer. "Where's my wife?"

Tisha must have heard my voice because she came running into
the foyer after me. "Eric!" she cried. "Let him through! That's her
husband!" she yelled at the cop who was only doing his job.

The policeman let go of me just as Tisha embraced me. Her hug
felt frantic and urgent, which made me panic even more. "Where's
Amber? Is she OK? What's going on?" I shouted as I pulled away from
Tisha's arms.

Tisha looked at me with sorrowful eyes, and I knew for sure that
the answer to my questions was something I didn't want to know.
"The baby," she said. My eyes widened as grief overtook my emotions.
Tears fell down from my eyes unapologetically as I sprinted further

into the house, running from room to room, trying to find Amber. I found her in her office. Paramedics had her lying atop of a gurney and were in the process of moving her out of the room and into an ambulance that was parked outside in the driveway.

"Amber!" I yelled. "What's wrong with her?" I demanded.

Amber was conscious, but the moment she heard me enter the room, she turned her face toward the wall and refused to look at me.

As they carted her way, one of the EMTs pulled me to the side and told me what happened, using a bunch of medical terminology. From what I could gather, Amber had been working in the office when she suffered a premature termination of the pregnancy. Basically, she had a miscarriage.

I looked down at the floor by her desk. Small pools of blood stained the already red-stained wooden floors. I wanted to stare at that spot forever, wishing my stillborn baby back to life. How could this happen? I knew. I had stressed her out. It was my fault.

"Mr. Hayes. Mr. Hayes!" the EMT called out to me, interrupting my self-loathing. "We're taking her to the hospital. She's okay, but it's standard procedure to take her to the hospital and have her receive medical care by a doctor. Do you want to ride with us there?"

I looked back down at the blood on the floor. "No. I'll meet you all there. Crawford Long?"

"Yeah. Just go through emergency, and they'll tell you where she's at," the EMT said before quickly exiting the room.

I was alone in the room with my guilt for less than sixty seconds when Tisha ran in. "You're not going with her?" she shrieked, tears pouring from her eyes. "Why not? She needs you? What kind of husband are you?"

That was a good question. *What kind of husband was I?* The kind that would lie to his wife, hang out late at night, partying with another woman, and allow the mother of my child to embarrass my wife in front of an entire courtroom of people: that's the kind of husband I was. I sniffled. "Tisha, I'm going to drive there. Please go with her and hold her hand through this. She needs her best friend."

She grimaced. I could tell that she was outraged. "But you're her best friend now, Eric! Don't you see that?"

I should have been her best friend, but I wasn't. A friend wouldn't treat another friend the way I had treated Amber. God told me to love her like I loved my own body. I had failed miserably. "I haven't been much of a friend to her at all lately. I can't explain it right now, but sometimes a woman should be with her female friends. There are some things that men just . . . we just can't be there for you like you want. Please, go with her. I will be there soon."

"But . . ." She blinked back fresh tears, nodded, and ran out of the door in an attempt to catch the ambulance before it pulled off.

Ten minutes later, I was driving my Chevy Impala to the hospital. The ride there seemed surreal as if I was floating on a sea rather than driving down the road. *The baby's dead.* The thought echoed through my mind like a scratched CD, playing on repeat. How could I have been so foolish? The last thing I ever wanted to do was hurt Amber and my child, but somehow, it was exactly what I did.

I probably should have traveled in the ambulance with Amber, but I really needed to be alone, at least for a few minutes. My face was wet with tears and being alone, I didn't have to wipe them away. I was crying for my strained marriage, for my wife who would have to say goodbye to her first child, for my baby who never got to see the sunrise.

It was sort of ironic that a year and a half ago I had come to the same hospital with Amber when her stepfather had a heart attack. She was engaged to Gold at the time, and I was extremely wounded that she had withheld her engagement from me, knowing how I felt about her. Now she was the one in the hospital, and I was the one who didn't tell the truth, but she had lost so much more this time than I thought I was losing back then. I guess life has a way of bringing us all full circle.

I waited in the waiting area with Tisha as Amber's doctor examined her and ran a few tests. During that time, I learned that Amber began cramping that morning and when it became hard to bear, she called Tisha who called 911. The emergency vehicles got to the house at the same time as Tisha and found Amber on the floor in her office. It was already too late.

When it was permissible for Amber to have visitors, I was called to her room and told that she was okay, but she had been given medicine to help her rest. I stood at the doorway, watching her sleep, appreciative that she was alive. I was also grateful that I wouldn't have to face her for a few more hours. No apology would be sufficient, no flowers, no card, no balloons; nothing would be enough this time.

She woke up and stared at me. Her eyes watered up, and I assumed she was thinking about our baby. I moved closer to her bed and took her hand into my own. I expected her to pull her hand away, but for whatever reason, she didn't. She just kept staring at me.

"Amber, I know that it's going to take some time for you to forgive me, and that's OK, but I want you to know that although I have failed you in many ways, I do love you and I do want this marriage. I promise you that I am going to stop trying to love you my own way, and start loving you God's way, with His love, because I know that God's love never fails."

I kissed her tenderly on her forehead and watched as salty tears streamed from the crevices of her eyes down to the white pillow below and thought, *God help us.*

Lesson 26: Do It For Heaven's Sake

Husbands, love your wives [be affectionate and sympathetic with
them] and do not be harsh or bitter or resentful toward them.

(Colossians 3:19)

"Brothers, we are basically down to our last class. Next week, we will
meet again to review all that we have discussed over these past three
months," said Minister Martin. "By now, you all may feel spiritually
exhausted, but that's good. God has been working on you and in you
throughout the class. You may have experienced tests and trials
during these months. You may have had to face fears and
unproductive thinking. Putting these lessons into practice may have
been challenging, but that is all a part of the process. God is refining
you; The Potter is molding you to be more like Him."

No truer words ever spoken. Exhausted didn't begin to describe
how I was feeling. I was completely broken. Everything that was
important to me had been flipped upside down. I felt like a loser, and
the word "lost" hung over my head like an annoying gnat. I had lost
my unborn child. I had lost the trust and affection of my wife. I had
lost my most lucrative business deal, and it was likely that I would lose
my custody case for my daughter. Yes, I wasn't officially down and
out, and there were certainly more things in my life that I could lose
before I bottomed out, but as much as I was hurting, I prayed that my
losing had come to an end.

I hadn't been back to work since Amber miscarried. Her doctor allowed her to come home the next day, and I took it as my responsibility to nurse her physically and mentally back to health. She lay in bed all day, fluctuating from sleeping to crying. Her appetite was non-existent so I had to force her to eat. She was severely depressed, and I was afraid to leave her alone for too long. Just to come to the Husband 101 class, I had to ask Tisha to come over and monitor her. Amber begged me not to tell her family or friends yet, so Tisha was the only person who came to help out. My family wanted to visit, but knowing Amber was in a delicate state, I asked them to just pray. It was the best thing anyone could do for both of us.

I considered playing hooky and not attending the Husband 101 class, but the class was ending soon, and with all that I was going through, it was essential that I be spiritually fed. I was weak, but participating in the classes was nourishing me in ways I had never expected.

"Before we go back to our original verses in Ephesians next week, I want to look at two other verses in the Bible." Martin flipped through his Bible as he spoke." Please turn with me to Colossians 3:17. We will be reading the seventeenth and nineteenth verses. 'And whatever you do, no matter what it is, in word or deed, or everything in the name of the Lord Jesus and in dependence upon His Person, giving praise to God the Father through Him. Husbands, love your wives, be affectionate and sympathetic with them, and do not be harsh or bitter or resentful toward them.' Once again, we, as men, are directed to love our wives. It is further explained as being affectionate and sympathetic towards them, as well as refraining from being harsh, bitter, and resentful in our dealing with them. This verse is consistent with what we've learned thus far in I Corinthians 13 and in Ephesians 5.

"But if we back up two verses, prior to husbands being instructed to love their wives, we all are directed to let everything we do and say be done in the name of Jesus, giving praise the Father through the Son. This verse appears directly before verses that discuss how wives, husbands, children, and servants should conduct themselves. Why?"

He looked around the room as if he was calling for a response from us, but no one was brave enough to answer his question so he continued.

"When we are living a life dedicated to God, everything we do must also be dedicated to Him. As we allow for God to abide in us and work through us, we become living sacrifices, vessels to be used by the Lord as He chooses. It is important that before we step into our roles as husbands, or any other role we may play, that we understand that we must first step into the role of worshiper. Worship is not just what you do on Sunday morning while the praise team is singing your favorite song. Worship is a lifestyle, a daily way to glorifying God in all that you do. Your life should be one of continuous worship. If so, loving your wife or any other command that He gives you will be as simple as breathing." Martin took a deep breath in and exhaled. He repeated. "Everyone, follow along with me and breathe."

We all began to take deep breaths and let them out. After we did this a few times, Martin asked, "Wasn't that easy? That is how easy worshiping God should be. That is how easy loving your wives should be . . . but somehow it's not. Somehow loving God and loving others is an uphill battle. We want to do it, but we fall short.

"Brothers, the reason why many of us struggle with love is because we have not completely laid down our lives before God. All that we do and say is not committed to Him. We want to give God pieces of ourselves, the pieces that suit us best. You can have this part of me, Lord, but I think I will hold on to the rest. God doesn't want a piece of you; He wants it all. If you find yourself having difficulty in loving others, examine yourself and assess whether or not you are committing your ways to the Lord, completely and wholeheartedly."

I nodded my head. As expected, Martin read me like a journal.

"And when you find yourself warring in your flesh, battling your own emotions and thoughts, remember that if you cannot show your wife love for her sake, you can still do it for Heaven's sake. People may not always be deserving of our love, but love does not seek its own. However God is deserving of not only our love, but our obedience. We must obey Him, and our compliance symbolizes our love for Him," Martin concluded.

Lesson learned. I had been giving God the pieces of myself that I wanted to give, not all of me. I still tried to hold on to my dreams and plans. The crazy part is that in His hands, my dreams and plans probably would have come true, but in my own, I tore down everything that was a part of the vision. He had given me so much including a wonderful wife and children. What man wouldn't want to walk a day in my shoes? But my joys weren't enough for me. I had to push for the achievements I thought I should I have. I couldn't just be grateful with the blessings from God.

The good thing about being broken by God is that once you surrender, there's no place to go but up. I would go back to court in two days to receive the verdict on Jonelle's custody case. I wasn't sure what the outcome would be, but I trusted that God would be with me. I knew it wasn't a coincidence that at the same time as I took the Husband 101 course, I was being tried in the areas of my life that kept me from being a better husband and man. I believed that God was sovereign and my steps were ordered by Him. He knew in advance what I would do, the mistakes I would make, and my desire to be redeemed. As I headed home that evening, I sang the song "Amazing Grace" aloud. I was a wretch who was saved by His grace. I imagined a man who had been blind for many years, going through a procedure that healed his eyesight. I considered how he would feel, what his experience would be like the first time he opened his eyes and saw what was in front of him. I could identify with that former blind man because for the first time, I was truly seeing what was in front of me, what I had overlooked and taken for granted for so long. In the car, I cried. Not out of pity for myself, and not for my heartbroken wife or unfortunate fetus, but in thankfulness to God for His grace. It was undoubtedly amazing.

Lesson 27: No Man Is An Island

Where there is no counsel, purposes are frustrated, but with many counselors they are accomplished. (Proverbs 15:22)

The day before the court ruling, Amber got out of bed and pulled herself back together as if the miscarriage never occurred. I wouldn't have believed it myself if I hadn't seen her with my own two eyes. I was sitting at the kitchen table, drinking coffee and reading the morning paper when she strolled past me, fully clothed in a hunter green pantsuit and heels, poured herself a cup of coffee, and walked out the door as if she were headed to work. I sat there perplexed, unable to comprehend how she jumped from mourning to business-as-usual overnight. Nevertheless, I didn't try to stop her. I was glad to have my wife back in the land of the living.

The day of the hearing, I was prepared to attend court alone. I sat in the courthouse next to my lawyer, silently praying the judge would rule in my favor. Lena was seated across the aisle from me with a smug look on her face while we waited for our case to be called. I kept asking God to help me to forgive her. I knew that if I held resentment towards her, it would only hurt our child and make a horrible situation worse.

Five minutes before our case was called, Amber walked into the courtroom and sat down beside me. Like the day before, she was dressed in business apparel and presented herself as if all was right in her world. When Lena saw her, the confident look fell from her face, and she pouted in displeasure. I tried to hold my demeanor so I didn't appear shocked to see Amber as well, but pretenses were no longer my strong suit.

"Amber, baby, I'm glad you're here, but . . . why are you here?" I asked, unable to refrain myself.

She continued to look forward as if she was paying attention to the case being presented, and whispered, "You're my husband, and I should be by your side, even when you mess up. Plus, there was no way that I was going to give Lena the satisfaction of thinking she had the power to split up our marriage."

I had always held the highest respect for Amber, but at that moment, I revered her even more, if that was possible.

I was about to smile when she added, "But don't think everything is fine because it's not. You and I, we are still not okay."

I should have seen that one coming. I had a good wife, but Amber wasn't to be taken lightly. I nodded and accepted the positive side of the situation. She was here with me, and that was a step in the right direction.

A few minutes later when my case was called, Amber stood next to me as the judge rendered his verdict. "This has been a very unusual case, I must say. However, I have reviewed both sides of the matter and have made a decision. It is my belief that every child should be given the opportunity to build a relationship with both of their parents, if that is viable. Although some questionable accusations have been made about Mr. Eric Hayes, none of these claims have anything to do with his capabilities as a father or his efforts to provide a safe, stable, and adequate environment for his daughter. On the other hand, Ms. Lena Henry has shown quite a bit of animosity towards Mr. Hayes, and her behavior reveals her intentions to keep Mr. Hayes not only separated from his child but also to sabotage his marriage."

"What?" Lena shrieked.

"Counselor Deere, please refrain your client from speaking while I am issuing my verdict."

"Sorry, Your Honor," Mr. Deere responded before hushing Lena.

"My decision is to grant Mr. Hayes joint custody as the primary custodial parent. Jonelle Hayes will be placed in the home of Eric and Amber Hayes effective immediately. Jonelle will spend weekends, holidays, and summers with her mother, Ms. Lena Henry. This case will be reviewed again in one year, and at that time, Ms. Henry can be reconsidered for primary custody. Child support payments will discontinue as both parents will be equally sharing the financial responsibility of the child. Ms. Henry, I encourage you to take this decision seriously and begin working on your relationship with Mr. Hayes so that you both can play an essential role in raising your daughter."

The judge's words struck me as his gavel made contact with the wooden sound block. I had been awarded primary custody of Jonelle. I had won. I couldn't believe it. I didn't know whether to smile or scream or do a victory dance. After all that had occurred during this case, I knew it was nothing but God's favor that was responsible for the ruling. How many good men who love their children had come into this same courtroom before me, minus the affair drama, and had lost their cases? There was no way that I could place the credit anywhere but Heaven.

Lena was completely devastated and required the help of her fake fiancé to help her exit the room. I was sure that she never imagined there would be such a turn of events. I turned and shook hands with my lawyer who also seemed surprised by the verdict. She shrugged her shoulders and said, "Well, congratulations, Mr. Hayes. Arrangements will be made to have Jonelle brought to you."

"Thank you so much, Ms. Greene. I appreciate all of your help," I replied sincerely.

"Honestly, I didn't do much. I spoke with your employee Carl and submitted his written testimony to the judge, but outside of that, I couldn't find much more to help your case. I guess the judge just saw the truth through the lies," she countered.

I shook my head. "It wasn't him, it was God. The Bible says it best: If God be for me, who can be against me?"

Ms. Greene smiled politely, offered a goodbye, and walked away. I could tell that she didn't understand. Like most people, she depended on herself rather than the Creator, but I couldn't judge her for it. Until recently, I didn't fully get it myself either.

I looked at Amber who had tears in her eyes. I knew why. She was happy for me, but forced to deal with the reality that although we were gaining a child in our home, it would not be the baby from her womb. She flashed me a bittersweet smile and kissed me on my cheek. "I guess I better get home and get the house ready for Jonelle. See you later."

Watching Amber walk toward the courtroom doors caused my heart to ache. She stood tall and confident, but I knew inside she was severely wounded. *How had we gone from being an ideal couple to couples therapy candidates?* I pondered the thought for a few seconds. Actually, it was exactly what we needed. I pulled out my cell phone and started to dial a number as I walked out of the courthouse and headed towards my office.

"Hey man! How did court go?" Carl said as he poked his head into my office an hour later.

I had been at the office all of thirty minutes, going through a pile of paper that sat in my inbox. I looked up at him and I continued to shuffle through its contents. "Terrific. The judge gave me primary custody of Jonelle. I'm still in shock about it."

"That's great news. I'm glad it all worked out." He stepped into my office and took a seat. I hadn't invited him in, but that was Carl. Besides, I still had yet to thank him for testifying on my behalf.

I tossed the papers back into the inbox. "Me too! Thanks for looking out for me and providing your testimony about Jay, I mean Ms. Johnson. I should have listened to you from the beginning."

"No problem. I know I joke around often, but marriage is like a war zone. You have to constantly be prepared to protect your relationship from forces that are determined to destroy it. I remember when I first got married. You talk about making mistakes? I was the king of mess-up! I would fall for every trick in the book. I can't count the times I slept on the couch or that my wife packed my bags and told me to get out. I was like, how you going to kick me out when I pay the mortgage?"

I laughed. "Carl, you're crazy!"

"I'm serious. It was rough. But over time and with the help of other men who knew more about how to stay married, I started getting the hang of it. I just had to learn to change my thinking. When

I was single, I lived life for myself. It was what I wanted, when I wanted it, and how I wanted it. It wasn't selfish; that's just how single people live, for themselves. They don't have to worry about anyone else, but when you get married and have a family, it's not about you anymore. Every decision you make impacts someone else. It cannot be your way all the time anymore, and that is what is really hard for most folks, changing their thoughts."

I thought about that he was saying. He was right. To a certain extent, I still was living for me and not my family. "That's real deep, man."

He chuckled to himself. "It really is. This one time, I think it was during my second year of marriage. I had been itching to get a new car. So I drove by this lot one day and thought I would just look around for the fun of it. That salesperson got to talking fast, and the next thing I knew, I'm driving home in a new ride. Got to the house and my old lady almost choked me out that night! No lie!"

We both began laughing. "Seriously?"

"She got straight violent. She told me if she ever saw that car again, I was going to be living in it. So I swallowed my pride and took the car back the next day. Never did that again!"

I shook my head and sighed. "See, when people tell me stories like that, it makes marriage seem like you're in prison, as if your wife controls everything. I don't want my marriage to be like that."

"No, my wife doesn't control everything, but when we got married we made a vow that two would become one. I can't make decisions, especially major financial decisions without including her and vice-versa. At the time when I bought that car, I knew that she had just lost her job and that money was getting tight. The last thing we needed was another bill. I made a selfish choice that wasn't beneficial for my family. She was right to demand that I take it back. The reality was that if I didn't return the car, we all could have been homeless eventually because we couldn't afford our house note and a new car payment at the same time.

"The thing is this, my wife isn't around to bring me down; she is there to help build me up. She knows my dreams and my plans, and a good woman is going to hold you accountable to the things that you told her you want to do. Like you and Amber. If you would have just told Amber what you wanted to do with the company, she would have helped you make it happen, but you were so busy trying to do it on your own that it all came crashing down on you. And in the end, she still had to fix things for you."

I raised my eyebrows. "What do you mean, 'she had to fix things for me'?"

"Oh, you don't know."

"Know what?"

He hesitated a moment before saying, "Amber came in here yesterday and made me tell her everything about Jacqueline. She took her file from your office, called a couple of connections she had first, and then called Ms. Johnson."

My eyes widened. "She called Jacqueline?"

"Yep. It was not a nice call either." He smiled and toyed with me, knowing I wanted to know everything.

"Stop playing games! What happened?"

He grinned at my frustration. "She told Jacqueline that she was contractually bound to use the realty and that she would sue her if she attempted to pull out and complete the sale with another company.

Amber also rattled off some people she knew and how displeased they would be to find out what Jacqueline was doing. Then before she hung up, Amber let Ms. Johnson know that if she ever approached her husband again, she would end up missing. Man, I didn't know your wife was such a gangster!"

I sat back in my seat. "Yeah, Amber can be a little scary. So let me get this right. Amber called Jacqueline and went off?"

"Let her have it."

"And now, we're still going to close on the Little Five Points property?"

"Yes. Well, I'm the one that's going to close on it. You have been banned from the deal, but you'll still get 75 percent of the commission."

"Who decided that?"

"The boss lady, who else? Amber Ross-Hayes. After the way she talked to Ms. Johnson, I was afraid to say anything to her except, 'Yes ma'am.' I think your wife needs a hug and some anger management classes."

I rubbed the back of my neck. "You're right about that hug. I've put her through a lot. I don't even know where her head is right now. She lost the baby, and I know she's—"

He jumped up out of the chair. "She lost the baby? Awe man! I'm sorry to hear that. That's why you've been MIA from work."

"Yeah. She's so mad at me. I don't know what to say to her."

He put both of his hands down on my desk and leaned against it. "I know that Amber loves you. You're just going to have to work as hard for this marriage as you do for this company. The same way that you don't build a business overnight, your marriage isn't going to work out perfectly overnight. Good, solid marriages take time and work. Just keep showing up every day, ready to invest yourself like you would do for your career. People put so much effort into their jobs, but they won't lift a finger for the people they love. We've got it all backwards."

I nodded. "You know, you would make a great marriage counselor. I think you missed your calling."

He sucked his teeth. "Trust me; I haven't always been this wise. These words come from experience. One day, you'll be able to pass down what you've learned too. No man is an island. We all have to help each other make it. Every person you see at the top has been helped by somebody to get there. There is no shame in receiving from others. Giving and receiving are what makes the world go around."

"Carl, you're right, my friend. And I'm willing to work. Matter-of-fact, I signed us up for a counseling session with the marriage ministry directors from her church. She might be mad that I did it without asking her first, but I wanted to show her how serious I am about dealing with our issues."

"I've been to marriage counseling before with the wife. Just remember to nod your head a lot and apologize about anything she says, and you'll make it out alive."

I laughed and threw a pen at him. "Carl, go back to work."

Lesson 28: Take The Lead With Love

However, let each man of you [without exception] love his wife as [being in a sense] his own self; and let the wife see that she respects and reverences her husband [that she notices him, regards him, honors him, prefers him, venerates, and esteems him; and that she defers to him, praises him, and loves and admires him exceedingly].

(Ephesians 5:33)

"Welcome, brothers, to the final class of the Husband 101 course." Minister Martin said. "I'm sure that it has been a life-changing thirteen weeks for the majority of you. I have prayed for each of you as you have taken this journey, and I believe that God has dealt with you all according to your individual spiritual needs. Growing up in the Lord can be challenging, but when you look back and see how far God has brought you from, the growing pains are worth it."

Several days had passed since my victory at court. Jonelle was brought to our house that same evening by a state social worker with only the clothes on her back. Amber and I spent the weekend purchasing clothing and personal items for her so that we wouldn't have to fight with Lena to send her belongings. Winter break from school was beginning at the end of the week, so Amber was driving Jonelle to school in the mornings until then. Because Lena was given custody for the holidays, Jonelle would spend her two weeks out of school with her mother and then return to us, the day after New Year's.

Jonelle seemed to be faring well with the judge's verdict. When I asked her how she felt about living with us, she shrugged and said that she would miss her friends who lived near her mom's house, but that she liked spending time with us. I was concerned about all of the adjustments she would have to make, but I was also relieved to have my daughter sleeping under my roof at night.

My relationship with Amber was still tense. She allowed me back into our bedroom only to save face in front of Jonelle. However, I was still forbidden from sleeping in the same bed as her and was forced to slumber on the pullout sofa on the other side of the room.

The day of the hearing, I came home and told Amber how I had scheduled an emergency couples counseling session with Minister Martin and Lydia. She was a bit irritated that I had made a decision without consulting with her first, but she was willing to go to the session as an attempt to work through our marital issues. We agreed to wait until Jonelle was staying with Lena over the holiday break before we met with Martin and Lydia, just in case our pending conflict took a turn for the worse.

Back in class, Martin was concluding our thirteen-week course of Husband 101. "I am handing back to you the paper you filled out on day one of the class when I asked you why you loved your wife. I want you to take time to read your answer again. There are no right or wrong answers, just your own. Once you've read what you wrote previously, I want you to ask yourself if this reason still applies. If your reason for loving the woman in your life is the same, write the word 'same' underneath what you wrote before, but if your reason has changed or evolved, write your new reason below the initial reason."

I read what I had written: I love my wife because when I'm with her I feel complete. She is everything that I'm not.

Although I still felt this way about Amber, my love for her and reason for loving her had grown over the past thirteen weeks. I wrote down beneath my old reason, my new one: I love my wife because she is a half of me and I need her to be the man I was meant to be. I love my wife because my relationship with her is a reflection of my relationship with God. As I grow closer to God, He fills me with His love, enabling me to love both myself and my wife, who is a part of me, more fully and completely.

Martin continued to explain. "Many of your views on why you love your wife have probably changed. The reason for this change is because you now have a clearer understanding of what love actually is and what it is not. It is hard to say why you love someone if you don't know what love really is, don't you think? As I said in the beginning, many people use the word love, yet their actions don't reflect anything that is loving. Once we truly understand the importance of love, what love looks like, and what love is capable of, it is much easier to identify love, who we love, and why we love them."

Once again, Martin was correct. Now that I had a better understanding of God's love, I was able to comprehend my own feelings of love. I could now see the people in my life that I cared for in a new light, in the light of God's love. His love seemed to be enlarging my heart, making it simpler to accept, forgive, and cherish those closest to me. I was no longer dependent on my own abilities to stay connected to them; God was now filling in the gaps where my own understanding failed.

"I want to go back to the Ephesians 5 and look at verse 33. It reads, 'However, let each man of you, without exception, love his wife as being in a sense his own self; and let the wife see that she respects and reverences her husband, that she notices him, regards him, honors him, prefers him, venerates, and esteems him; and that she defers to him, praises him, and loves and admires him exceedingly.' I am ending our time with this verse because I want you all to see the result of your loving. When you are obedient to God and you love your wife, wonderful change can occur in your marriage. Notice that the verse starts off requesting that men love their wives, but ends elaborating how women are to respect and reverence their husbands.

"My conclusion is this: When you take the lead with love, you set your family in order, and propel your wife to submit to you and respect you the way you desire her to as a man. Fellas, you no longer have to try to control your wife or force her to treat you like a king. All you have to do is love her with God's love in you; that's it. The Bible tells us that if we seek the Kingdom of God and His righteousness, His way of doing things, everything else will be added to us. It's time for us to step into our positions as men, putting order back into our homes, and it starts with love. When we set the example and lead with love, the various aspects of our lives will begin to line back up in their proper place, but we've got to make the first move. We've got to make the choice to love. Now that we understand this thing called love, let's embrace it, live in it, and lead the way with it."

Ending the Husband 101 course was bittersweet. I was glad to be getting my Mondays back, and I felt a sense of accomplishment by getting through all thirteen classes despite my personal issues, but at the same time, I had begun to really appreciate the weekly spiritual guidance and brotherhood. I knew that moving forward, I needed to participate in a group Bible study or commit to individual devotional time to replace the encouragement I had been getting over the past three months.

Martin ended the class with a group prayer. "Father God, as these men continue on in their lives, help them to remember Your Word and the lessons that have been taught during this course. Allow them to experience Your love on a daily basis and to reflect that love onto their wives or girlfriends, children, families, and out to the world. Honor them for their dedication to becoming better husbands, fathers, and men. Lead them in their decision making and teach them how to be role models for others to look up to. Let each of them keep another accountable to doing what is pleasing in Your sight and never be so full of pride that he is blinded to his own shortcomings. Let us all work out our own salvation with fear and trembling. As we close out this course, we recommit our lives, marriages, families, careers, and dreams to You. We decrease so that You can increase. Let Thy will be done. In Jesus' name we pray, Amen."

Lesson 29: Falling Is Easy, Getting Up Is The Challenge

For a righteous man falls seven times and rises again, but the wicked are overthrown by calamity. (Proverbs 24:16)

Because of his work schedule, Martin and Lydia were unable to meet with Amber and me for the emergency counseling session until the morning of Christmas Eve. While we waited, living in the same house as Amber was pure torture for me. My love for her had grown deeper than ever before, but our unresolved marital issues created an impermeable wall between us that I didn't know how to knock down. We were cordial with one another and spoke when necessary, but outside of these bare minimums, our communication was nonexistent.

I kept asking myself, *How did we get to this place? How do two people who love each other so much end up on opposite sides in a battle?* Amber was my best friend. Not being close to her was as if I were on the outside looking in at my own life; I felt helpless and lonely. It was easy to see that her love for me was still strong. She had not left me and continued to support me as a wife should, but our connection was missing and I went into our counseling session praying that this intervention would somehow re-solidify our bond.

Lydia had prepared for us a special Christmas Eve breakfast, filled with Belgian Waffles, eggs, sausage, fresh fruit, coffee, and orange juice. At first, I was a little confused about why we were eating breakfast in the midst of a crisis, but I went along with their itinerary.

Martin blessed the food and the four of us began to eat, making small talk along the way. Once Martin had devoured half of his waffle, he put down his fork and said, "I know you two may be wondering why we are eating breakfast? No, it's not because Lydia likes to feed everyone that comes to our home—which she really does enjoy doing. One thing I've noticed about people over the years is that we tend to connect during mealtimes. For some strange reason, when food is present, things get real. Meals can bring us closer or they can reveal the things that are tearing us apart.

"Lydia and I do some basic marital and premarital counseling with the church, but we don't consider ourselves therapists. We don't have educational backgrounds or training in psychology, so we don't profess to be in a position to work with people on an ongoing basis as it relates to their therapeutic needs. Nonetheless, we do view ourselves as marriage advocates and educators, and we are committed to mentoring younger couples as we have been mentored by those who preceded us." He nodded at Lydia who continued his speech.

"We asked you two to breakfast so that we can talk like friends instead of like therapists," she said. "We are not exactly sure how we can help you, but when Eric called Martin and asked for marriage counseling, we didn't want to turn you away. Martin sensed that you both needed guidance and support."

Martin added, "We are telling you all of this in advance so that you both have realistic expectations of the outcome of this meeting with us. We want you to feel free to share with us what you all are going through, and as friends, we will offer you feedback, prayers, and biblically-based resolutions, but we will not attempt to conduct intensive therapy with you. If that is what you two need, we can refer you to some excellent Christian marriage therapists that we know. Is that OK?"

I glanced over at Amber who nodded her head. I also nodded and said, "Thanks for clarifying that for us. I wasn't sure what to expect from us meeting today, but it helps to know what will and won't happen."

Lydia took a sip of her coffee. "We have learned after working with several couples in this capacity to be upfront and honest so that people don't feel let down if we do not uphold their preconceived ideas about our time with them." She took another sip, and said, "So, who wants to tell us what is going on?"

Amber set her eyes on her barely eaten waffle and refused to look up. I took that as a sign that she wasn't volunteering to speak first, so I began to explain. "Well, the last few months have been difficult for us as a couple. We were expecting our first child, but there were some medical risks associated with the pregnancy and the doctor wanted Amber to take it easy. However, some of the decisions that I made ended up stressing her out, and a few weeks ago, Amber miscarried. I know that she is hurting about losing the baby, and I am also very saddened by it."

I continued to stare at her, but she would not return the favor. "In addition to that, I was so determined to develop the real estate company that Amber gave me that I became entangled with a female client who was interested in me. Nothing happened between us, but I did withhold information and lied to Amber about the situation. Unbeknownst to me, my daughter's mother, Lena, had hired a PI to follow me around. This person took pictures of me with this client, and Lena presented them in court as if I were having an affair.

Because I wasn't completely honest, I don't think Amber trusts me anymore. I feel that she loves me and doesn't want our marriage to end, but she's put up this fence around her heart, and I don't know how to make things right between us." Finishing my statement and feeling exposed, I shoved a forkful of scrambled eggs into my mouth.

"Amber?" Lydia encouraged.

Amber looked up from her plate and made eye contact with only Lydia. "Eric summed it up about right."

"So what do you think about what he said. How are you feeling?" Lydia probed.

Amber sighed. "I'm afraid that if I say what I want to say that I'm going to hurt his feelings. I've worked really hard at trying to be a wife who is good to her husband and does not tear him down with my words. You all know that my mouth has been a weakness of mine in the past, so I am not sure if it's a good idea for me to talk about what I think and feel."

Lydia smiled. "You really did learn a lot during Wife 101, Amber. I'm glad to see that some of the lessons stuck with you. But right now, it is important that you communicate with your husband. You cannot just shut down out of fear of hurting him, because not talking to him will hurt the both of you more. I understand that you want to be gentle with your words, and you should be. Try this: Say how you are really feeling, but whatever you say, say it the way you would want it to be said to you. Most of us do not like to be spoken to harshly, even if what is being said is the truth. So tell him how you feel the way you would want him to tell you how he feels if the situation were reversed."

Amber peered at Lydia who nodded her head in reassurance then shifted her eyes to me. "Uh . . . Eric, I . . ."

"Go on," Lydia prodded.

Amber huffed. "Eric, I can't believe this is happening to us so soon in our marriage. I feel like I was completely wrong about you. I thought I knew you, but then this whole mess makes me wonder if I even knew you at all. I mean, yeah, you claim that you didn't cheat on me, but you lied to me which makes believing that you didn't step out on me so hard to believe. How could you take off your ring for another woman? Then when I asked you about it, you made up some crazy story! I knew that your story was suspicious, but I didn't want to be that kind of wife who second guesses everything her man does. Now I *am* that insecure woman who always wonders if what you're telling me is true! Each time you leave, I question you in my mind; where are you really going? Are you going to see Jay or some other chick? Yes, I'm hurt! But I don't blame you for the baby dying. At first I did, but I knew the pregnancy was risky. For some reason beyond my understanding, God allowed the baby to die. Neither you nor I could have prevented it."

"I'm hearing both positive and negative words and emotions," Martin intervened. "Eric is taking responsibility for what he did to cause problems in the marriage and is trying to relate to how Amber feels. Amber is recognizing her pain and mistrust towards Eric, but also is not pointing the finger of blame on him for everything that has gone wrong. This is good. Marriage is two people working together. When problems arise in marriage, it is rarely one person at fault. Both parties usually influence the issues, and often external people and forces also play a role."

Tears began to well-up in Amber's eyes and I felt awful about how badly she was heartbroken. "Baby," I said. "I am so sorry that what I did made you feel insecure. You don't ever have to feel unsure about my love for you. I don't want to be with anyone else. Even when Jay was coming at me, I never liked her. I never wanted to be with her. I told her about you, that I loved you. You have to believe me because it kills me to know that you think I would want any other woman but you."

She threw her hands up in the air, obviously in frustration. "How can I believe you, Eric? You know how mad you were when I didn't tell you that I was engaged to Gold and we weren't even together back then. After that, we promised to always tell each other the truth no matter what. When you didn't tell me about Jay and let me believe she was a man, that was jacked-up. But when you told me that bold-faced lie about why your ring was on the wrong finger; how can I believe anything you say after that? You didn't even blink or stutter when you lied to me! You said it so easily as if this is something you do all the time! I never blatantly lied to you. Even when you came home and Gold was at the house, I was always upfront. Actually, that was one of the reasons he came to the house because I didn't want to meet with him behind your back. I wanted you to know about our business discussions, regardless of the fact that they had nothing to do with you. I didn't want to keep any secrets from you. You were late coming home that day, but if you had come home on time, I would have been able to tell you he was stopping by, and it wouldn't have been a surprise to you. But, no! You got there late and started acting as if something's going on with him and me. Meanwhile, you were really the one out having secretive meetings and partying and living it up with some other chick!"

I grabbed one of her free hands and held it tightly. "I was wrong, Amber. I know I was wrong. I admit I was wrong. All I want to know is how to make it right."

She yanked her hand away from me. "I don't know, Eric! Maybe you can't make it right! Maybe the damage is already done, and we can't go back!"

Her words felt like a slap across the face. A few tears fell from my eyes as I imagined a life without her. "Please don't say that, Amber. Please baby. I know that what we have is real, and it's special. I know with God's help that we can fix this. You just have to forgive me. You just have to let it go."

"Let it go?" she asked. "Seriously? Eric, you are such a hypocrite! So you want me to forgive you and let it go, but I'll put money on it that you haven't forgiven your father for cheating on your mother yet! You haven't let that go, have you? It's OK for you to hold onto that, but I'm supposed to be so understanding when it comes to you?"

My eyes widened at her accusation. I couldn't respond. She had thrown my situation with my father in my face, which was agonizing but true. I wanted to forgive my father, and somewhere in my heart I did, but I had not made amends with him. As far as my father was concerned, we were still at odds. Deep down, I knew that the reason I had not cleared the air between him and I was because it was my way of making him suffer a little longer. Amber knew me better than she realized. I didn't want to be punished, but I wanted to punish others. My pride and self-righteousness had become my demise. I wiped the fallen tears away and new ones formed in the cervices of my eyes.

"Eric," Martin said. "Do you know what Amber is talking about? Is there mending needed in the relationship between you and your father?"

I nodded, tears choking out my voice.

"I know this is hard for you, Eric," Lydia replied, "but Amber has a point. We cannot pick and choose when mercy should be extended. If we want others to forgive us, we must forgive those who trespass against us. Can you tell us what's going on between you and your father?"

I picked up my glass and swallowed some of the orange juice to help myself calm down. I felt so vulnerable crying in front of Amber and the Woods, but if opening up would save my marriage, now certainly wasn't the time to act tough.

"My dad," I began, "I found out not too long ago that my father cheated on my mother and produced a child from the affair. It happened before I was born, but my mom just learned recently about the affair and the woman who says she is my father's daughter. I was so devastated. I thought my family was different from all of the other broken families out there. I looked up to my dad. I wanted to get married and have a family just like my dad, but when I heard about the affair, it crushed me. I do forgive him because I love my dad, but I haven't told him yet that I've let it go. I guess I didn't want to make it seem like what he did was OK. I wanted to make him suffer a bit so that he would know how much he let his family down."

"How do you think I feel?" Amber cried. "Don't you think I feel the same way? That I don't want to forgive you because I don't want you to think that it's OK to do this? I'm scared out of my mind that if I let you sweep this Jay thing under the rug that sooner or later you'll do the same thing or worse again because I didn't make you suffer enough this time."

Martin wiped his mouth with his napkin and intervened. "It sounds to me that both of you are trying to control another person using guilt. Eric, you want your father to feel guilty about his affair, and Amber, you want Eric to feel guilty about lying to you. Both of you seem to believe that if the person at fault feels bad enough, they won't commit the offense again. Contrary to your beliefs, people don't stop their behavior because of guilt; they stop because they have changed. Eric, if your father is a different man now than he was back then, he won't cheat on your mother again. And Amber, if Eric has really learned from this incident, he will be more upfront with you from now on. Both of you need to realize that you cannot control others or manipulate them into change; you have to leave them in God's hands and trust Him to work out their shortcomings."

Lydia passed both Amber and me tissues. "If you all really want this marriage to survive, it's time to learn one of the best but more difficult lessons that I had to learn in my marriage. Falling is easy, it's the getting up that is the challenge. In a relationship, you will find that problems will come, and they will come so easily. How easy is it to get into an argument? How easy is it to disagree? How easy is it to become irritated or annoyed? How easy is it to make an error in judgment? It's so simple; it's so easy. But resolving an argument, agreeing to disagree, turning frustration into peace, and righting wrongs are the challenges. Yet it is when we are able to face these challenges with single mindedness and a determination to stay together that we overcome, that we return to a standing position. Each of you is going to have to decide if you're going to be fighters or flee-ers. When times get rough, are you willing to fight for the marriage, or are you going to let the issues pile up until fleeing through divorce is the only option? You've got to choose now because this won't be the last time you'll be forced to get back up after time and chance have knocked you down. It's all a part of life, and it's all a part of marriage."

"Lydia's right," Martin said. "This is a good time to decide how you two as a couple will deal with obstacles. Are there any other issues that either one of you want to put on the table while we are getting it all out and in the open?"

I shook my head no, but Amber spoke up. "Yes. I'm not trying to be a complainer or seem jealous, but as much as I love my husband's family, I am tired of him always running to them every time there is a problem."

"Hunh? What are you talking about?" I asked in disbelief.

"Eric, plain and simple, you're a momma's boy." Amber said boldly. "It's like you haven't learned to let them go and be a family with me. You depend on them way too much, and it gets in the way of you depending on me. Every time something happens in our home, you jump in the car and race over to your parents' house to talk to your mother. I know you guys are close, but I'm your wife; you should be talking to me. The Bible says that a man leaves his mother and father and cleaves onto his wife. You refuse to leave and cleave. I've never said anything outright because I thought that our marriage was new and maybe you were still adjusting, but it has been almost a year, and I know you, Eric. Tell me that you didn't run down to your momma's house after the blow-up in court. Tell me you didn't. Say it, Eric."

I felt attacked, blindsided by her assessment of me and my relationship with my family. "Yeah, I went to see them, but they were waiting on the verdict, too. I had to tell them what was going on. Plus you told me to get out of the house!" I said defensively.

She sucked her teeth. "I told you to get out of my face. That didn't mean you had to leave the house! You could have gone for a walk or went upstairs or went back to work! You didn't have to go running to your parents. You're a grown man, Eric. Stop acting like a child who needs his mommy! Be a man and realize that being with me is where your home and obligation should be, not with them. You won't even go to church with me half of the time because you have to be at church with them. Do you want to be married to me or married to your momma?"

Married to my mother? That was a low blow; her words cut me like a sharp dagger. "Wow!' I exclaimed. "I didn't know you felt that way."

She looked me square in the eyes and said, "Well now you do."

Neither of us spoke for several seconds, so Martin regained control of the conversation. "I know you both are feeling emotional, so expecting you to leave our home with resolution is unrealistic. I want to ask you both to try something that might help. Go on a 5-day fast. I understand Christmas is tomorrow, so wait until the day after and then fast for the 5 days before New Year's Eve. For each for the 5 days you are fasting, go 5 hours without eating, and during those 5 hours, pray at least once an hour. Don't make any decisions about your marriage while you are fasting, simply talk to God about it, and let Him talk back to you. On New Year's Eve, come to our anniversary party together, and by the end of the night, decide what you want to do. This way, you will come into the New Year knowing how to proceed with your marriage. Old things will be passed away and all things will be made new. Agreed?"

Amber and I looked at each other, pain still filling our eyes. "Agreed," we said in unison.

Lesson 30: No Place Like Home

He who finds a [true] wife finds a good thing and obtains favor from
the Lord. (Proverbs 18:22)

Over the next week, I spent a lot of time alone, praying and thinking.
So much had been said during our meeting with Martin and Lydia that
caused me to re-evaluate myself, my relationship with my wife, and
my interactions with the other people in my life who affected me, like
my parents and Lena. Amber's words to me were not easy to swallow.
I wanted to deny her accusations, reject her feelings, and dispute her
views, but the reality was that nothing she said was invalid. Yes, I
hadn't truly forgiven my father yet, but I expected her to forgive me
without a second thought about it. Yes, I leaned too much on my
parents, especially my mother, and I often felt more obligated to my
family of origin than to my wife. Yes, I wanted Amber to be honest and
forthcoming with me, but I wasn't always willing to return the favor.
Truth be told, I was surprised that she hadn't called me out about my
chaotic relationship with Lena. I had some ironing out of emotions
and behaviors that needed to be dealt with regarding her too. With all
of the chips stacking up against me, I followed Martin's directive of
praying, fasting, and communication with God.

Carl had reported that Jay's closing had been a smooth process. I
stared at the hefty commission, acknowledging that the majority of my
recent life drama had stemmed from the overwhelming desire to get
that one check. Was it all worth several added zeros in the bank? I

shook my head in shame. No amount of money was worth the repercussions of this one deal, but it was done and over. My goal moving forward was to appreciate the business that I owned and allow God to increase it as He saw fit. If Hayes & Ross Realty remained a small company that dealt primarily in residential properties, that was fine by me. If God decided to bring companies and organizations our way like the contacts I had set up in January that was fine, too. Either way, I had been blessed and favored to be on the receiving end of a good company with a great reputation, and I would never again allow my own selfish ambition to threaten what I had been blessed with.

New Year's Eve

The day before New Year's Eve, I ended my fast and was certain of the next steps that I was to take. The morning of New Year's Eve, I left the house early. I had a few errands to run before attending the Woods' anniversary bash that evening.

My first stop was to Lena's house. She opened the door with her house robe on and messy hair, looking at me as if I were the tooth fairy.

"What are you doing here?" she asked, confusion, surprise, and a hint of anger in her voice.

"Sorry to spring up on you without calling, but I really needed to talk to you."

She stepped out onto the porch and closed the front door behind her. "Well Jonelle is inside, and we are having a good time together, so if you are about to say something that's going to make me upset, I would rather not have this conversation with you."

I smiled. She always thought the worse of me; that was why we could never get along. "Lena, I didn't come here to argue with you or make you upset. I came because I need to apologize to you. We had a kid, and although we were not able to make it as a couple, our child still deserves to have parents that can model maturity to her. We don't want her to grow up thinking that how you and I treat each other is how women and men should act. I've played my role in our disagreements, and I accept responsibility for my mistakes. It's time for us to bury the hatchet and do right by each other and Jonelle."

I moved closer to her and gently placed her left hand inside of both of mine. I expected her to pull away, but she didn't. "I am sorry for anything I have done to you during our relationship and since then that has hurt you, offended you, or made you feel that I don't appreciate how well you've taken care of our daughter. You've been a really good mother to her and you have made a lot of sacrifices for her. I am not blind to any of the good things you've done. When I took you to court, it was not about me feeling that you weren't doing a good job; I just wanted to be involved in her life as well. We are going to have to learn how to share her and not to use custody as a way to control or get back at each other."

Lena blinked a few times and nodded. "OK. I'm sorry too . . . for keeping her from you."

I didn't anticipate her having a big speech like I did. I was willing to accept anything positive she was willing to give. I let go of her hand and pulled her into an embrace. She didn't really hug me back, but she didn't get mad and shove me either. Some people I would just have to be patient with. "Thank you," I said to her as I removed my arms from around her and began to walk away. She stood there in front of her house watching me as I got into my car and started it up. I waved at her. She waved back and then headed back into the house.

An hour later, I found myself sitting across from Jonathan Gold in his office on Peachtree. I certainly had surprised him with my unexpected visit, and I could tell that he was nervous of what I might do.

"Jonathan, can I call you Jonathan?" I began. He nodded, and I continued, "I wanted to come down here and give you my blessing to work with my wife on the community service your company wants to do at Sunrise Sunset Daycare. I am sure that after your last meeting with Amber back in October, she halted any discussion of it. Am I right?"

"Yes, she told me that she didn't think it was a good idea" he said.

I leaned forward. "It wasn't that she wasn't interested, she was just trying to respect me. She knew that I wasn't comfortable with you being around her. What man would be comfortable with his wife's ex-fiancé being around? I'm sure you feel me."

"I can relate," he replied. He was looking at me as if he were trying to figure out where I was coming from. He didn't trust me which was understandable.

"I now recognize that not only can I trust Amber, but I have to allow her to make business decisions that will be best for her company. She has worked very hard to build these endeavors, and if she believes that the service project your company is proposing will help the people she serves, I don't want to stand in the way of that. If you all are still interested in working with her, I would suggest giving her a call after the New Year and re-presenting the idea to her." I stood up and offered my hand for a handshake, a truce.

"Oh . . . OK. Thanks. I appreciate your visit," he said while accepting my hand and shaking it firmly.

"No problem. Happy New Year." I turned to exit his office.

"Eric, I mean, Mr. Hayes?" he asked, causing me to stop and turn back.

"Eric is fine."

He grinned authentically. "Good. How did you know I would be at work today?"

I shrugged. "People like you and Amber never miss an opportunity to work."

He laughed. "You have a point. Thanks for coming by."

I picked up a few more things that I needed for the evening's event, including my dry cleaning then headed to my last stop before returning home: my parents' house. I knew my parents were planning to attend Watch Night Service at church that evening, which was a family ritual. For the first time in many years, I would not be with them. No, I would be with my wife at the Woods' anniversary party.

"What are you doing here so early?" my mother asked when she saw me walk into the living room. "Where's Amber? You're not planning to go to church with that on, are you?"

My father was sitting in his blue Lazyboy recliner and looked up at me long enough to give me a head nod of recognition.

I sighed, trying to figure out how to let my mother down easily. "Amber's at home. We're not going to church with you all tonight."

"Oh, you're going to her church?" Nessy asked with disappointment in her tone.

"No, Mom. We are actually going to an anniversary party tonight that's being hosted by a couple of the members at her church. You remember the Husband 101 course I was recently taking? The teacher of the course and his wife are renewing their vows tonight."

"On New Year's Eve? What kind of church does she go to?"

"Amber goes to an excellent church, and starting in the New Year, I will be moving my membership to her church."

Neesy leaped up from the sofa. "What? You can't do that? You grew up at First Christian Church!"

I rubbed my mother's arm to try to calm her down. "I know, but I'm married now, and it's time for me and my wife to be as one. We shouldn't be in separate congregations. She has made a lot of sacrifices for me, and I think this is a sacrifice I need to make for her. I really like her church, and I think it will be a good place for Jonelle and our future children."

"Eric!" Nessy cried.

"Mom, I know you don't understand, but I can't be a child here with you and be a man at home with my wife. It doesn't work. I have to let you guys go and lead my family now. That's what Dad did for us, and that's what I have to do for my family."

"He's right, Nessy," my father intervened. "You have to let him go and be a man. He's grown now. Baby, you got to let him move on."

Nessy nodded her head in compliance and left the room. I knew my mother was heartbroken. I was her baby, her youngest child, and letting me go meant accepting that all of her children had left. My father was with her, and I was certain that he would comfort her and help her adjust to a truly empty nest.

"She'll be OK, Son," my dad said. "I'm proud of you for doing what you have to do for your family. That's what manhood is all about."

I sat down on the sofa in the spot where my mother had just been. "Dad, I also need to talk to you, too. I need to apologize for the way I've acted about the whole affair situation and let you know that I've forgiven you."

My father stood up and walked over to where I was sitting. "You don't have to apologize; I am the one that made the mistake, but I thank you for letting me know that I'm forgiven. I hated knowing that I disappointed you so much."

"I was wrong too. I held a grudge against you just to punish you. Worst part about it, I wasn't the most righteous person myself. I'm truly sorry, and I want you to know that I still respect you and look up to you. I still want to be as good of a husband and father as you."

"Be better than me, Son."

"I'll try." We hugged as a sign of love and release. I spent a few more minutes with my father, talking to him about sports, family, and whatnot. As I was preparing to leave, I asked, "So, what about Denise? What are you going to do about her?"

He chuckled. "I've actually spoken with her a few times on the phone. She is going to come to Georgia next month so that we can meet her. We are going to get a paternity test just to make sure, but I've seen her picture, and I know she's mine. I hope when she comes, you'll come out and meet her."

I smiled and nodded my head. "Definitely. She's a part of the family."

Amber was so beautiful that evening that I had to force myself to stop gaping at her. It was crazy that I had risked my closeness to her over some foolishness. I couldn't stop touching her, and I knew she was ready to slap me because she said so. The Woods' anniversary bash was held at a banquet hall in Gwinnett County. White lights and candles filled the space giving it a romantic and magical feel.

At 11 PM, Mr. and Mrs. Woods renewed their vows. It was a short, but charming ceremony that would cause even the biggest critic to believe in true love. Following the ceremony, I led Amber out to a private balcony that overlooked the property's massive garden. The scene was picturesque, and I hoped it would help us commit to spending our lives together.

"Amber," I said while taking a hold of both of her hands. "A lot has happened between us in the past few months, and most of it has been my fault. I've spent the past week fasting and praying, and God has really confirmed for me that being with you is where I want and need to be. You were right about so many things. It's amazing how you know me better than I know myself. I am so blessed to have someone so special who loves me so much as my wife.

"I had a busy day today. I talked to Lena, and we are going to try to start being more cordial with each other. I also talked to Jonathan Gold and gave him my approval for him to work with you on his community service initiative."

"You what?"

"Let me finish. I made up with my father. I needed to do it because my resentment was hurting the both of us. He's a good man, and he didn't deserve how I was treating him. And . . . I also let my mother know that it was time for me to separate myself from them and to be more present with you. So in the New Year, I will be joining your church, and I promise to stop leaning on them so much. I want to be the head of this family I have with you. I want to be your husband and your covering. I want you to trust me and believe in me like I trust and believe in you. I want you to forgive me and love me and give me another chance."

By the time I finished talking, tears were pouring from Amber's eyes. She sniffled and tried to wipe them away. "You're making me mess up my makeup," she said.

I pulled her into my arms, "I'm sorry, baby."

"I am too."

I squeezed her tighter. "Do you forgive me?"

"Of course, I forgive you. Love never fails."

I leaned back and looked into her eyes. I was mystified. "What? How did you know?"

"Know what?"

Had Martin told her the lessons of Husband 101? "Love never fails."

She giggled. "It's in the Bible, Eric. Somewhere in Corinthians. I do read the Bible, honey, and I attended the Wife 101 class. But I also know it because I know how I feel about you. I won't pretend that forgetting is going to happen overnight, but I'm willing to work towards it."

That was Amber. I was so glad that she knew what I knew. We were really meant for each other. "I'll take that. I love you so much."

In the distance I could hear the party attendees counting down the New Year. "10 . . . 9 . . . 8 . . . 7 . . . 6 . . . 5 . . . 4 . . . 3 . . . 2 . . . 1, Happy New Year!" they screamed out. I leaned down and kissed my wife, the love of my life. It was already a happy new year for me.

Epilogue

Lesson 31: And Life Goes On

Life is in the way of righteousness (moral and spiritual rectitude in
every area and relation), and in its pathway there is no death but
immorality (perpetual, eternal life). (Proverbs 12:28)

Valentine's Day

We stood hand-in-hand in a gazebo on a hilltop that overlooked the
vast Atlantic Ocean. Small waves crashed against the rocky beach then
retreated back to join the seemingly endless sea. It reminded me a lot
of the past several months; something beautiful ending up in a stony
place, but through the grace of God, able to return back to its original
greatness.

We celebrated our first anniversary in the Dominican Republic,
finding peace and reuniting our love on the private beach of a
luxurious resort. After all we had been through as a couple, we both
agreed that we needed a vacation, and the D.R. was one of the
Caribbean islands which neither of us had ever been to before. The
decision was an excellent one. It was time to move on and enjoy the
precious gifts of life and love that God had blessed us with.

Still holding my hand, Amber took a step forward and released the
white rose she was holding. It fluttered through the air, passed the
shoreline, and into the turquoise-colored sea. We watched it land

gently on the watery bed and slowly float into the distance. When we could no longer see it, she turned to me and exhaled. The flower represented so many things to us, mainly our unborn child. We were releasing its memory to God and trusting Him to give us another chance at parenting when He saw fit.

Tugging on her hand, I drew her back to me. Although there was no music playing, I began to rock her from side to side, letting nature be our orchestra. After several seconds of dancing, I dipped her, kissing her sweetly before bringing her back to a standing position.

"You know you're really corny, right?" she said, completely ruining the moment. Only Amber.

I let out a phony frustrated grunt. "Woman, I swear! You just don't have a romantic bone in your body, do you?"

"Nope, but thank God, I have you to balance me out. And I like corny; it meshes well with crazy," she said, smiling affectionately at me.

"You're right. You know I'm a sucker for crazy." I stared into her dark brown eyes. "Happy Anniversary, Mrs. Amber Ross-Hayes. Thank you for not giving up on me. I love you."

She smiled again. "Giving up on you would mean giving up on me, and I refuse to do that. We're in this for life. I love you, too." Her smile was authentic, and so were her words, but in her eyes I could see the small glint of pain that lingered. Life would go on, but healing would take time.

I pulled her closer and kissed her again. If I ever had any questions about us, they no longer existed. I knew that with her was the only place on this earth that I ever wanted to be. Our relationship was still far from perfect, and I was aware that it would never be flawless, but that was what made it uniquely ours. There were unresolved issues, and we were both willing to address them in the days to come, doing whatever it took, including signing up for a couples retreat that our church was hosting in August. We were sure that if God was guiding Martin and Lydia to lead it, attending would only strengthen our marriage. Thankfully and prayerfully, we had made it through year one. God willing, there were many, many years left to come.

The Husband 101 Workbook

Experience the novel Husband 101 firsthand with The Husband 101 Workbook. This co-ed, interactive, study guide by Author and Marriage & Family Educator, Dr. A'ndrea J. Wilson, takes both male and female readers beyond the novel and into the actual Husband 101 course. Take a deeper look inside the 31 lessons of the book, the 13 verses of I Corinthians 13, and the 13 classes that make Husband 101 an unforgettable novel. Follow along as Eric and his classmates are challenged to become better men, husbands, and fathers. Get a richer understanding of the role of a man and how the Word of God directs men to think and behave. Use The Husband 101 Workbook as a part of your church group, book club, or in your personal quiet time.

AVAILABLE NOW AT DIVINEGARDENPRESS.COM

Wife 101 & The Wife 101 Workbook

Mess or Mrs.?

Thriving Atlanta mogul Amber Ross thinks she is the perfect woman. But when she finds out that her recent ex-boyfriend is marrying someone else, she begins to question what men really want. Frustrated with the dating scene and her failing interactions with men, Amber enrolls in a course at her church geared towards teaching women how to be effective in their relationships: Wife 101. Amber expects the class to shed some light on her courting flaws, but it does more than that; it challenges many of her life choices and ideas about romance. Her new attitude brings unexpected love, but has she learned enough to make the right choices and snag a great husband, or like a foolish woman, will she tear down her home with her own hands?

Also look for The Wife 101 Workbook in paperback

Final Exam Question #3

Can six couples with a boatload of issues survive on the hottest beach in the USA?

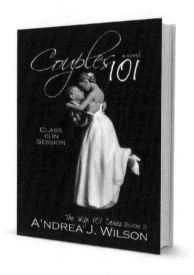

DIVINE GARDEN PRESS

...redeeming marriages and families one book at a time.

WWW.DIVINEGARDENPRESS.COM

DIVINE GARDEN PRESS INTRODUCES

Janell

Thrillers for the Soul

WWW.IAMJANELL.COM

About the Author

A'ndrea J. Wilson, Ph.D. is the author of Wife 101, Husband 101, My Business His Way: Wisdom and Inspiration for Entrepreneurs, The Things We Said We Would Never Do, the Kiss & Tell: Releasing Expectations, Grave (from the Love Said Not So Anthology), and the Ready & ABLE Teens Series. She has also co-wrote the song "Pink Hat Day" which appears on Inspirational Singer, Carmen Calhoun's I Am CD. A lover of education and learning, Dr. Wilson has earned a Bachelor's of Science in Psychology from the State University of New York, College at Brockport, a Master's of Science in Counseling Psychology; Marriage and Family Counseling from Palm Beach Atlantic University, and a PhD in Global Leadership; Educational Leadership from Lynn University. She currently divides her time between writing, conducting relationship and professional development workshops, and teaching college courses. In addition to writing, Dr. Wilson is the President of Divine Garden Press, a publishing company which promotes books that address marriage and family issues. A'ndrea currently resides in Georgia.

Book Clubs & Reading Groups:

Visit www.husband101.com for a printable reading group guide